EMMA'S JOURNEY

America has long been at the heart of Emma's dreams, especially now her oldest and dearest friend, Bea, has decided to live there. When Emma's husband, Paul, is approached to take part in a lecture tour, an impossible wish suddenly seems to have been granted. As she sets sail on the Queen Mary the journey proves far beyond even Emma's expectations and the luxurious life in Washington is all too easy to grow accustomed to, but first impressions can be misleading. When Bea's youngest son Mark goes missing, Emma finds herself helping her friend in a desperate and heartrending search...

EMMA'S JOURNEY

EMMA'S JOURNEY

by

Elizabeth Daish

Magna Large Print Books
Long Preston, North Yorkshire,
BD23 4ND, England.

British Library Cataloguing in Publication Data.

Daish, Elizabeth
  Emma's journey.

  A catalogue record of this book is
  available from the British Library

  ISBN   0-7505-1473-6

First published in Great Britain by Severn House Publishers Ltd., 1999

Cover illustration © Melvyn Warren-Smith by arrangement with
P.W.A. International Ltd.

The moral right of the author has been asserted

Published in Large Print 2000 by arrangement with Severn House
Publishers Ltd.

Magna Large Print is an imprint of Library Magna Books Ltd.

Printed and bound in Great Britain by
T.J. (International) Ltd., Cornwall, PL28 8RW

One

'You must be really thrilled, Sister.' Eileen fingered the tussore silk and lace angel tops and sighed.

'I find it hard to believe that Bea can go into a shop in Washington and buy whatever she wants for the twins, and presents for us.' Emma Sykes put the rest of the small garments on the highly polished chest of drawers in the bedroom and handed a smaller parcel to Eileen. 'She sent this for you,' she said and smiled, hoping that her face didn't look as stiff as it felt and that her voice was warm.

Eileen tore off the wrapping paper and held up a garishly embroidered dress, perfect for a baby girl – if one wore dark glasses and lived in the hotter parts of the United States of America. 'Mrs Miller, you are a lovely lady,' she breathed, looking heavenwards as if in prayer. Eileen glanced at her employer and seemed embarrassed. 'Are you sure you wouldn't like to exchange this for one of yours? It's so beautiful.' She hugged the dress as if she couldn't bear to part with it but thought she must try to be fair, as the plain and elegant cream tussore silk seemed to her to be dull against the bright embroidery.

'Quite sure,' Emma reassured her firmly. 'Mrs Miller knows that you like bright colours.' She could imagine Bea choosing the clothes, knowing exactly what each of the young mothers would prefer, and trying to hide her own preferences. The bright dress must have caused her some misgiving, but seeing Eileen's almost tearful eyes, Emma knew that as usual Bea had got it just right, however much she might have shuddered when she bought the gaudy dress.

'I wish she would come back,' Eileen said sadly. 'We all miss her, don't we, Sister?'

Emma's tense face relaxed. She had forgotten that it wasn't only her who missed the friend who had played a major part in her life for several years; they had trained together as nurses during World War II at the Princess Beatrice Hospital – Beatties – in south-east London. There was so much that was both good and bad to remember of that time, and later, during their fairly light-hearted period as private nurses. That was before Bea had taken her twins and followed her husband Dwight to America, then had another son Mark; and before her own little Rosamund had been born at Beatties over two years ago.

'I'll get Mick to take a snap of Jean in the dress. It's a bit big for her now but she'll grow into it soon and it will last all the summer. He can take one of Rose as well,' Eileen offered. 'That new camera is wonderful and he fancies himself as a photographer.'

'I'll go up to the consulting room while you find Mick. I promised to sit in when Esme Bolt is under hypnosis. She should be gone by four and we can have tea and buns at half past.'

Almost wearily, Emma climbed the stairs and tidied the large airy room where Paul saw his psychiatric patients. She picked out two wilting daffodils from a vase and smelled the earthy fragrance of the tiny iris bulbs in the wide blue bowl. Spring again and Rosamund was a potent reminder of new life and growth, but Emma was tired. On the way to help her husband she had looked in the nursery and gazed down at the sleeping child, now quiet but gathering energy for the next burst of fun and games. Such energy, and Emma found it difficult to keep up with her now that she was walking and eager to explore.

'Is she having her nap?' Paul asked and grinned.

'At last! I nearly climbed in beside her. I had no idea that one small girl could be so exhausting.' Paul regarded her with a wry smile. 'I know I should be glad to see all that activity, or so my psychiatrist husband told me, but compared with Jean, Rose is hyperactive.' She smiled and glanced towards the door as if she might be overheard. 'Not that I'd change her for Jean. She's prettier and so healthy that I want to eat her at times.'

'You need a rest. You help in the clinic and do nearly everything for Rose as well as organising the house. We must find a girl to share the load. No, don't protest! I don't want a wife who is limp and sad. Now tell me what is wrong; not Rose or the hard work but something more.'

Emma moved away restlessly, almost upsetting the flower arrangement. 'It's nothing, or almost nothing. I find that spring is always a trying time, and this year it's worse, now that we are emerging from winter, and yet it's not warm enough to let Rose play in the park.'

'Is that all?'

Emma looked uncomfortable. 'This may sound as if I'm envious, and I suppose I am. Bea sent one of her in-between-birthday presents and a very good letter and I suddenly felt low. There is nothing I can send her that she hasn't at least two of and the shops here are so lacking in goods. Will these shortages ever go away? She casually talks of treats that the twins enjoy as routine and Mark has so many toys that Bea gives away those he discards when he is tired of them. They have this wonderful nanny who wants to stay for as long as Bea needs her. It's a bonus that Bea says the girl is partly British and she has no really sharp American accent so the twins still sound at least half British.' She saw Paul's quizzical expression and sat down heavily on the leather chair by his desk. 'All right Doctor, I confess. I have a fit of the blues. I miss Bea as much now as I did after they went back the last time that Dwight brought her over here.'

'So you need more than pink pills for pale people,' Paul said.

'I don't need a tonic at all.' Emma yawned. 'I just want to walk up the road and see food shops with no anxious women holding saggy string bags outside the butchers and with newspapers ready to wrap up the bread. It's become a habit since they rationed bread for a while after the war. We thought that once it was over we would be back to what we knew, but there seems to be a kind of grey apathy as if we have shortages and must put up with them for ever. Bread rationing is over now thank goodness, but when that happened I thought we'd really reached rock bottom! We didn't even have bread rationing during the war when the convoys were bombed and our own farms produced less grain than we needed.' She shrugged impatiently. 'I know we did well and we had a supply of flour from one of your farmer friends, so we could make soda bread and scones and real bread when I could find yeast; but most people had so little and I felt guilty accepting extras that they couldn't obtain or afford.'

'So you made soda bread for the cleaner and most of her large and hungry family.' Paul laughed. 'I noticed that the whole house smelled of baking for weeks, but it was a good idea.'

'It was the least I could do.' Emma brushed aside any hint that she was too generous.

'Bea misses you, too,' he pointed out. 'All that luxury can never take the place of friendship, but Bea is in the right place,' he added firmly. 'She couldn't settle here again as her life is with Dwight and the babies and she does enjoy the American way of life, but there are times when Dwight is worried and wishes we were there.' He eyed his wife thoughtfully. 'I worry about you at times but you are in touch with your roots and can talk to Aunt Emily and Janey and visit places you will always love. I know you couldn't tear yourself away from all that and we couldn't be apart for more than a holiday.' He put a finger under her chin so that he could see her eyes and looked serious. 'Could we?'

Emma put his hand to her cheek, felt the flow of love between them and shook her head. 'I *am* happy, but sometimes I know I could do more. Not more in the house, sitting in the clinic or looking after Rose – that is true fulfilment – but I have other talents and they are a bit rusty.'

'You said you couldn't go back to Beatties, even after being asked to do so several times.'

'Not that, but I miss the sensation of being able to make someone better, or at least to bring relief and hope to ill patients. Wasn't it Milton who wrote about "Having one talent that is death to hide, lodged with me useless..."'

'You do enough here, but I know what you mean.' Paul glanced at the wall clock. 'Miss Bolt is late but I think I hear Mick with her now. We must talk again later, Darling. I get far too absorbed in work and time flies, but I do have an idea or two that might help. I don't think it's Eileen's evening for the flicks so we can go out to Mario's and talk seriously over a meal and a bottle of wine. Mario said he'd save a bottle of Rioja for us.'

'Lovely.' Emma's cheeks dimpled and she was relaxed. 'I promise not to leave you alone with Esme Bolt; that's if she hasn't seduced Mick on the way up.'

'She *is* getting better, but please don't leave me.'

'Some men would enjoy having half the nymphomaniacs in London chasing them.'

'Very funny!'

'She's very pretty.'

'Too many men have thought so. I have the result of the Wassermann and it's positive.'

'Syphilis?' Emma whispered, he nodded.

'I want to find what triggered her obsession with sex so we'll have a fairly deep session today and then I have to tell her what's wrong clinically and refer her to Davies in 'A' Block at Beatties for treatment.'

Emma giggled, remembering the uncompromising attitude of Dr Davies and his thick Welsh accent imbued with the disapproval of generations of Welsh Chapel. 'What a challenge for Esme!'

'Quite a challenge for Davies! I almost believe that he does that particular job with venereal diseases to punish himself for something.'

'Maybe he needs a good shrink,' Emma whispered as the door opened to admit Esme. Mick Grade hovered behind her ready to escape as soon as possible, his face slightly red.

'Ask your wife if we can have tea in about half an hour,' Paul said solemnly, to impress Esme with the fact that Mick was married and unavailable.

Esme stared at Mick and smiled. 'I do hope you haven't married a *good woman.*

What a waste of a good strong body,' she purred and Mick nearly fell backwards from the room.

'I hope you've kept the diary up to date,' Paul said. She nodded. 'And the drugs?'

'I've been quite good, but I know you won't think so,' Esme replied sulkily. 'That medicine tastes absolutely filthy and makes me so sleepy that I don't feel like having any fun.'

'That is the idea,' Paul said simply. 'You lost two very good jobs because you embarrassed your employers, and your own doctor asked me to help you. I need to find out what caused your condition, so that you may be able to control your ... urges.'

'It wasn't fair. I ran that shop well until the wife of a customer complained that her husband was meeting me after work.' Esme was the picture of innocence.

'And the other job?' Paul asked.

'That was a bit naughty I suppose, but it takes two to tango.'

'On the office desk?'

'It's so difficult, Doctor. I seem to have wonderful jobs offered to me as I *am* pretty and very efficient but there are a lot of very attractive men about. I can work really well unless I'm distracted.'

Paul consulted a folder on his desk and Emma saw that Esme was eyeing his well-set shoulders with far too much interest, so she led the woman to the couch and helped her off with her shoes and jacket before settling her down comfortably.

Paul held a syringe up to the light and expelled a small bubble of air from the liquid. 'Just to relax you into a light sleep.' Emma rolled up the loose sleeve and swabbed the patient's arm with a wad of gauze moistened with surgical spirit and then held the hand steady while the needle slid smoothly into the vein. A piece of sticking plaster was placed over the syringe to secure it in place and allow the plunger to be depressed whenever Paul needed more thiopentone released into the vein.

Esme smiled. 'This is wonderful. A sort of floating feeling almost as good as gentle sex.'

Paul refused to have eye contact and told her to take three deep breaths. 'Just think back to when you were completely happy as a child.'

Esme closed her eyes and relaxed her grip on Emma's hand. 'It was so long ago. It was before I went to school.'

'Were you happy on your fifth birthday?'

Esme giggled. 'Had a party and we all played sardines. I hid in a cupboard and my uncle found me and said he wanted a reward for being clever in finding me so quickly. He said we must keep quiet and he gave me a big hug.' Paul put her slightly deeper and she sighed. 'He had soft hands and he stroked me all over, then kissed me. He was kind and said he loved little girls.' She wriggled lower on the couch. 'Daddy never said he loved me, not once, and when I was all spotty with the measles, he pushed me away when I wanted him to hug me and told Mummy to keep me away from him as I was hot and smelly, but Uncle Robbie said he'd sit with me and read a story while Mummy went to the shops, and he took off my nightie and rubbed me all over with scented powder. It was lovely and my skin was cool.'

'You loved Uncle Robbie?'

'Yes but Daddy was nasty to him and he went away.'

'What happened?'

'It was Christmas and we'd undone our presents and I went to sit on Uncle Robbie's lap but Daddy said I mustn't.'

'Did Uncle Robbie live with your family?'

'He stayed with us very often and always brought me nice presents and we had a secret.' She laughed. 'He was silly, really. I liked what he did to me but he told me that if I said anything to Mummy, she'd be cross and he'd go away and never come back.'

'Did he ever hurt you?'

'Not really hurt. Only once after he'd given me some nice orange juice and I couldn't really stay awake. It hurt a bit but after that once it was nice and I asked him to do it again the next time he came to us.' Esme began to cry. 'But Uncle Robbie went away. Why did he go away? I tried to snuggle up to Daddy as I did to Uncle Robbie but Daddy pushed me away and asked me whether Uncle Robbie had touched me and hurt me. I said I loved Uncle Robbie and he loved me and I hated Daddy for being so nasty.'

Emma saw the tension in Paul's face and she held the patient's hand gently. 'So Robbie went away,' Paul said softly.

'Daddy hit him and I was frightened and tried to hug Uncle Robbie, but Daddy smacked me and sent me to bed, and the next day Uncle Robbie was gone and there was nobody to make me laugh and to love me. Daddy said I was wicked and I must never let anyone do those things to me again or God would punish me.'

'So you tried to find Robbie?'

'I ran away three times but I never saw him again. I looked everywhere and tried to find someone like him but I never did.'

Paul injected a little more thiopentone and Esme breathed deeply. 'Think about later. Were you happy at school? Was it a girls' school?'

'Yes. I was quite clever and good at sports. When I was twelve we had a new games master. He was like my uncle. He had fair hair and his eyes laughed and made me want to be near him.' Her voice became more adult. 'He was a creep. He said he loved me and we did make love but he was no good and he went with other girls, so I wouldn't let him do it again, but I was so lonely, until we had to join the boys at the grammar school for science, and I tried to find someone like Robbie there.'

'And you've never found anyone like him?'

Esme gave a shuddering sigh and tears fell again. 'Sometimes it's very good and I'm happy but afterwards I feel so lonely that I drink too much and I have bad dreams.'

'When you wake up you will take your medicine and enjoy being sleepy. You will think of good things that have nothing to do with sex and the next time someone wants you, be sure that you really like him as a person and not just for the act of sex.'

Esme sighed and yawned and slowly sat up. 'Was I asleep? It was good. What happens now? Do I go on with that horrible medicine? Someone told me it was like the bromide they gave to the soldiers when they couldn't have women.'

'It is a bit like that,' Paul admitted. 'I hear that you have a new job?'

'Another shop. At the trial interview they liked the way I dressed and my easy manner with customers.' She grinned. 'Not the male customers, and I'm being very discreet. I'm glad you told me that I am sick, Doctor. I thought I was a freak who ought to have been a prostitute. I do draw the line there. I sleep with men who are clean and nice-looking.' She glanced up and saw Paul's expression. 'What's wrong?'

'One of your men wasn't clean. I had the result of your blood test and you have a rather unpleasant sexually transmitted disease.' Paul spoke seriously and without emotion and Esme stuffed a handkerchief into her mouth to stifle her sobs. 'I shall write to a colleague at the Princess Beatrice Hospital who will treat the disease. If you have any regard for others, you will not have intercourse with anyone until you are cured. This is a notifiable disease and the law could intervene if you knowingly infect another person.'

'What can I tell my friends? I'd hate to have this made public.'

'You will attend a clinic but your name will

be confidential and you will answer to a number. If anyone asks if you are receiving treatment there they will be unlucky as your name will be only in the records and not on your chart.'

'One of those VD clinics? It sounds like prison. Must I go there?'

'Now you have been diagnosed, you must be treated. The sore that you reported to your doctor is highly infectious and the sooner you have drugs the sooner you and any sexual contacts you make will be safe, but the fact that you can be cured fairly easily now with antibiotics, compared with a few years ago when the treatment was tedious and often took several months, does not mean that you can never be re-infected. This is not an immunisation against further infection.'

Eileen tapped on the door and Emma asked her to come in. She put the tea tray on the desk and eyed Esme with interest before leaving the room again. 'Why didn't you want to take the tray, Mick?' she asked when they went down to their own apartment.

'Go near her? Not on your Nelly, and

26

you'd better be careful when you do the washing up.'

'What a thing to say! I thought she looked nice but a bit shocked. She was very clean and smartly dressed, Mick. She doesn't need a doctor for something catching. Dr Paul isn't that kind of doctor. He treats the mind and the nervous system.' She smiled. 'That suit must have cost a lot. Did you see that lovely scarf?'

'I saw her notes,' Mick said briskly. 'The blood test was positive.'

'What test?'

Mick regarded his wife with pity mixed with amusement. 'A blood test to see if she's been a naughty girl and caught syphilis.'

'Who could do that to a nice woman like her?'

'The doc will be more concerned as to how many she's given it since she got her dose,' Mick retorted severely.

'I don't believe it.' Eileen's eyes widened. 'You don't mean she's a prostitute?'

'Na! Nothing so common! She just likes sex and they don't need paying if she fancies them, which is most of the time.'

'I can't think that I'd fancy many other men,' Eileen said. 'I find you quite enough!'

'You'd better keep it like that, my girl,' Mick said grimly, but slapped her bottom gently, and she giggled.

Two

Mrs Coster was, as usual, washing the hall tiles when Esme left.

'She can't bear to miss anything and she seems to know when there's any drama in the consulting room.' Emma laughed. 'I think she'd love to listen in to your hypnosis sessions and she tries to winkle out details from Mick if he's been sitting in as chaperone during a consultation.'

'She probably thinks she knows as much about the human brain and its functions as I do, but she does push her luck at times even though her rather earthy common sense is impressive.' Paul poured more red wine into Emma's glass and smiled. 'She's been with us ever since we came here and we'd be lost without her, so I hate to upset her. What was her diagnosis this time?'

Emma sipped her wine and then looked roguishly over the rim of her glass at her husband. 'She told Mick to watch out as "that one" was a right tart. She'll probably warn you too, given the chance.'

'She knows better! As Mick is ex-service, Mrs Coster takes it for granted that he was tempted by women who haunted the camps and probably slept with one or two, but I doubt it. Mick came from a poor background but had enough sense to distance himself from such entanglements. His sister was an example of what he might become if he stayed with his family and played the black market, or worse. It took a lot of hard work and dedication to become a sergeant with a lot of authority.'

'He was much more help to us when he was in a wheelchair than any of the orderlies, and he took over a lot of our paperwork as he does here.'

Paul looked pensive. 'We depend on him a lot, and he handles the office work better than most trained secretaries.'

'I'll never forget how he managed my mother's affairs when she died and I had the flu and couldn't cope with the funeral,' Emma said fervently.

'I want to make clear what our future will be here with Mick and Eileen,' Paul said.

Emma looked startled. 'They haven't hinted that they want to leave? Eileen is happy as our housekeeper and they both love their nice comfortable apartment. Little Jean is sweet and is company for Rose and we share the baby-sitting so that Eileen can indulge in her twice-weekly visits to the cinema and I can feel free to leave Rose in safe hands whenever we need to be away for a few hours.'

'Don't panic,' Paul said mildly. 'I admit that life is orderly and good but there comes a time when we have to do other things. I have been unwilling to alter anything, but as you know, I have turned down a few offers of lecture tours and decided that it would be impossible to leave here for a long holiday or business trip.'

Emma sat very still, aware that something momentous was about to happen.

'I want your help and honest opinion before we decide anything. If you want to stay here and go on as we have done, I shall say no more about it.' He laughed, suddenly boyish. 'But I think you will find my pro-position interesting, Sister!'

If he was Guy, Emma thought suddenly, recalling her lover who had died helping the survivors in Belsen, he wouldn't have asked me or considered my opinion on anything important – he would have *told* me after he'd arranged it and expected me to agree. 'What is it? And what have Mick and Eileen to do with it?' She smiled. 'You bring me to Mario's and ply me with delicious food and wine and soften me up for what?'

'Would you like to visit Bea? Take our time over there while I do two lecture tours?'

Emma burst into tears and Luigi, Mario's son, hovered anxiously by the next table. 'Tears of joy I hope,' Paul said hastily and Luigi beamed and rushed away to the kitchen. 'You do realise that he is telling his wife that you must be pregnant again?'

Emma laughed through her tears and took a deep breath before drying her eyes. 'Luigi is convinced that tears of joy must mean another *bambino*, but usually it's the wife who knows first, not the husband, and I'm not.'

'Very coherent,' Paul said. 'So they might just be tears of joy?'

She nodded and her voice was husky. 'It's a dream. I hoped it would come true but at times I couldn't think that far ahead and it made me sad, but is it any closer now or is it still a dream? There's the clinic and your patients, the house and Rose.'

'A hundred things,' Paul said happily, 'and we have enough help and support to see to everything.'

Luigi glanced disapprovingly at the wine in Emma's glass and Paul held out the empty bottle. 'If you have another like that, we'd like it. Join us if you have time, Luigi. My wife is *not* expecting a baby but we do have something to celebrate.' Luigi's face cleared and he came back with a fresh bottle and sat with them, hoping to hear more.

'America? I have a brother in New York who wants me to go there and open a restaurant with him but I am here with an English wife who hated the Yanks during the war.' He shrugged. 'I am content and I think she would not like my brother, or I would not like him looking at her as he does with other men's wives, so I stay here where I am not jealous and you bring all your friends here, yes?'

'If we go away, I'd like you to have some money to pay for anything that Eileen orders if they have to feed visiting doctors. She will have enough to do without catering for parties. When the money is used up ask Mick to pay you, as he will handle the day-to-day expenses.'

'Will there be visiting doctors?' asked Emma. 'What about the clinics? Where will your patients go and who will look after them?'

'The clinics will continue with a locum psychiatrist in charge, and possibly an assistant.'

'Have you brought him here to eat, this new doctor? Is he *comprensivo* ... sympathetic and easy?'

'That's a problem I have to face. I have two men in mind who are clever and seem very well qualified, but I haven't decided which one to approach first.'

Luigi grinned. 'Invite them to eat here and my wife will tell you who is the right one.'

'I think I need another opinion, Luigi, and there are things such as qualifications and references to check,' Paul said lightly. 'You can't judge a psychiatrist by the way he holds his fork or drinks his wine.'

Mario chuckled. 'My wife would know as soon as he lights a cigar or cigarette. There was a man who wanted her, before she married me, and she said he was charming and wanted to be *amoroso* but as soon as he struck a match and lit his cigarette she knew him to be bad and dishonest with women.'

Paul roared with laughter. 'She was joking, Luigi. I have never seen that one in any of my textbooks. How could she know?'

Luigi looked deflated. 'She would never say it to me.'

'But she married *you*, Luigi,' Emma said consolingly. 'You can tell her from me I know exactly what she meant. I saw a lot of men in hospital who gave a clue to their real characters over quite small mannerisms.'

The two men stared at her in disbelief. 'What a good thing I don't smoke,' Paul said cryptically. 'What happens if I bring him here and he doesn't smoke, either?'

'Then you leave him to me and Aunt Emily.'

'The lady from the Isle of Wight who visited you and showed my wife how to make light, light cake?' Luigi kissed the tips of two fingers and sighed. 'A wonderful lady who told me I would have a son, and Antonio was born safely after much labour.'

Paul tried to be serious. 'I don't think that this is the way to appoint a senior psychiatrist for six months, with a view to a partnership later.' He began to laugh again. 'Poor man, if I confronted him with you and your wife Luigi, not to mention Aunt Emily, and, of course, our Mrs Coster who cleans the house and makes spot judgements on all who pass her over the wet hall tiles.'

'Don't forget Mick and Eileen and *me*,' Emma retorted.

'Maybe I should leave you to it for a week and come back when you've made a decision,' Paul said dryly.

'You would want to book a table, Doctor?'

'I'll let you know!' Paul replied weakly. 'I wish I'd never mentioned it here.'

Luigi helped himself to more wine and

36

filled the other glasses. '*Salute e fortuna.*'

'And may he be acceptable to our loyal friends, Mick and Eileen,' Emma added.

'Who are at this moment in charge of our daughter and may want to get to bed. Stop dreaming and get your coat.'

'I take it that you have put in a toe and found the water not too icy?' Emma said as they walked home.

'If you mean, have I made any progress towards finding a suitable locum, yes I have, and I was surprised that at least four people showed an interest. Two have wives and children and might be bad choices as far as Mick and Eileen are concerned. The children in both families are at least ten or twelve years of age, and noisy. I dropped in to see them casually and quite honestly I'd hate to let them rip in our house. Both of the doctors believe in self expression and I'd not want them expressing themselves all over our drawing room.'

'Mrs Coster would leave at once! What about the others?'

'The others are both unmarried and younger. One said he was now in Dublin, after having worked in Edinburgh for a year or so, but some of his family live in Surrey so he'd like to be near them for a while. Half a year would be fine for him, living in the house and carrying on the practice very much as I run it as far as psychoanalysis is concerned; but he isn't a neurologist. He was with a group of doctors at the last meeting we had at Tommies but none of the others knew him when I tried to find out more about him.'

'And the other?'

Paul glanced at Emma and hesitated. 'He's ex-service – Navy – and has done locum jobs for the past year. He's met your cousin George and likes him.'

'I'm not surprised. George is a very likeable man,' she said firmly. 'He is going to be married again. Remember the nice Wren officer he met in Inverness? Aunt Janey says that she gets on well with George's son Clive and she wants more children to make a complete family. It's what George needs and I have great hopes for them.'

'Will she leave the service and take care of Clive?'

'Not really. I know that Clive is very young but George thinks he's nearly old enough for boarding school and he wants to go away. Living with his grandmother all the time and attending a very small school where they don't have decent sports fields can't be much fun for an active boy. George has very limited time with him as he's in the Navy, so school is the answer and it will give George and Margaret time together. Until he is ready for boarding school, Clive will stay with Janey as he is now, and then come to her for holidays and half-term breaks later when George and Margaret will be able to see him there.'

'As Clive doesn't remember his mother and has been secure and loved living with Janey and Alex since just after he was born, the future looks good for him, with few hang-ups,' Paul said, drawing on his professional expertise.

'Margaret and George have mutual friends and she knows the Navy, which helps. Poor Sadie was out of her depth with George's friends and homesick for America and her fashionable life there.'

'And George was still in love with you, Emma.'

Emma brooded for a full minute then said quietly, 'I think he's forgotten me but I'm not sure. As there was never anything going between us, at least as far as I was concerned, and we are first cousins, he had to find someone to fill his life after Sadie died and I married you. If we are really truly going away I want to miss their wedding. I have no intention of being even the faintest of spectres at the feast. It's only fair that Margaret can have her husband to herself and wipe out any thoughts of me for ever.'

'Wise girl.' Paul tucked her hand into his and kissed her on the cheek.

'So when do I meet the candidates?'

Paul frowned. 'I hate to make it difficult for you but when we were all talking and George was mentioned, I asked Commander Forsyth to come over for dinner, purely for a social occasion as I knew you'd be interested in meeting him.'

'And what happened?'

'Dr Allen was listening and asked if he was included as he definitely wanted to be interviewed for the possible locum job. I told him that this was not an interview but he said that he'd need to come to see me soon to discuss the possibility as he was very keen to join us. He hinted that I was giving Forsyth an advantage because we had a mutual friend.' Paul looked embarrassed. 'He made it sound as if I had rejected him before he had a chance to tell me about himself and was, I thought, a bit offended. I remembered that we invited Catharine and her husband to dinner and you said you might ask the Sister from Beatties so I thought that he could be invited to make the numbers even. He has a certain charm and socially would be fine, but if both candidates were there together with me, a perfectly good social evening might become nothing but shop talk.'

'Is he professionally sound?'

'Who can say on such a brief meeting? But as I felt obligated, even though I haven't advertised the post as yet, I've asked Martin Allen to dinner tomorrow if that's okay. The ex-naval type can wait until the later date I arranged with him and maybe the others could come to that party, too.'

'Fine. With Robert and Catharine and Sister Joan Bright from Casualty at Beatties, that will make a good mix. Joan can look them over. She's a great judge of possible talent, medical and romantic. I'd better make sure she can arrange to be off duty to come to dinner with the other one too, so that she can compare.'

'Why not just line up the Inquisition and parade the candidates before them? I'm glad it isn't me! Imagine Mrs Coster's beady eyes boring into me while Eileen and Mick mutter between themselves and Joan Bright asks awkward questions. Terrifying!'

'I'm not terrifying and I'll make sure he feels at home. He might terrify us. If he takes the practice I hope he likes Victorian beds with brass knobs.'

'You'd put him in Bea's old room?'

'We'll be coming back and I want our rooms left as they are. He can have that bedroom and the dressing-room for a private sitting-room and a spare room for guests, but leave our rooms alone. The office and consulting rooms will be enough as they are and Eileen will still queen it over the kitchen and allow him to use the drawing-room if he wants to entertain, with food brought in from Mario's or whatever he likes to arrange, so long as she is not over worked. As it is, Eileen and Mrs Coster will have to do the shopping that is normally my job. I wonder what Mick will say?'

'He will look after our interests and I trust him completely to handle the financial business and the bookings. In the old days on large estates, he would have been the steward and have a lot of power. Maybe we are not so big a concern, but the idea is the same – steward, keeper of the keys, major-domo? Which do you think he'd like to be?'

'They will need a rise in wages.'

'That's easy. We are quite well off now and the offers I've had for the lecture tours are very generous.'

Emma slipped out of her winter coat as soon as they entered the house and warmed her hands by the sittingroom fire before checking that Rose was asleep.

'The scourge of physical examinations is cold hands,' Paul said. 'Rose wouldn't appreciate being held unless your hands were warm. That should be taught as priority to every eager student and embryonic nurse.'

'I learned the hard way,' Emma admitted. 'We had a convoy of six old people bombed out of a Home, and when they were put into bed, hardly knowing that they'd been moved, let alone bombed out, I thought one of the old dears was dead as she was so pale and limp and I could see no chest movement. I put a hand under her nightie to feel her heart and she slapped my wrist and said very crossly, 'Take your ruddy cold hands off me!' I was very embarrassed, but not as much as the chaplain who came in later to set their spiritual minds at rest and who was asked in ringing tones for the piss pot, my lad, and be quick or I'll do it in the bed.'

'Nursing lets you meet such refined people.'

Rose was asleep, her small fingers curling over the sheet and her mouth slightly open. Emma brushed aside a heavy lock of dark brown hair and kissed her gently. Not light

44

brown hair like Paul; but her eyes had his steady gaze and were as tawny as his, the slight gold flecks making them bright; yet people seeing her for the first time said she was like her mother.

Mick answered the in-house phone, connected at night to buzz quietly and flash a light instead of tearing away the silence and disturbing the whole house. 'Good grub?' he asked. 'There were a couple of calls for himself. Nothing urgent except that a Dr Martin Allen said he could manage to come to dinner tomorrow but would like to come over a bit early before dinner to discuss the work here.'

There was silence for a few moments, then Emma asked for details of the other call.

'What's up, Sister?' Mick asked bluntly. 'It sounded as if Dr Allen wants to work here. Is there something I missed? Going away and selling up, are you?'

'You'd be the first to know if we had to do that, Mick,' Emma said tactfully. 'Nothing like that; in fact we might have to expand and have a locum to help out if Paul goes on a lecture tour, but it's pie in the sky as yet

45

and I heard about it for the first time this evening. Nothing has been discussed and certainly nothing will be decided until we have a meeting with everyone connected with the clinic. We'd want to know a lot about anyone we had to trust to take over any of our clinics and our home, so we may invite a few likely candidates socially to assess how well they'd fit in here.'

'I knew that the doc wouldn't pull a fast one, but I was a bit worried. This Dr Allen is to be given the once over? Sounded as if he already had his feet under the table.'

'Paul will assess their capabilities as psychiatrists but we'd depend on you and Eileen to make your frank assessments as anyone working here will affect you. However skilled they may be, the one who comes here must be, as Mario or Luigi would say, *sympatico,* and a warm person. I hope that Dr Martin Allen isn't taking too much for granted as at least four people were interested when Paul mentioned it at the last congress in London, even though he told them that there is nothing planned for the immediate future.'

46

'That's why he was so keen and a bit pushy,' Mick said. 'Wants to get his foot in the door first. How long would you be away? If the lectures didn't take a lot of time, he could live out and come in for clinics.'

'I really know as little as you do, Mick, but I was given a hint that we might go to America.'

Mick gave a low whistle. 'What a turn up! But about time. I'll keep it quiet and not tell Eileen tonight, as she will worry, but you know that we'd sort out any problems from our point of view. Tell the doc I'll come up to the office after breakfast before I do my phoning. I'll chivvy up the plumber. That tap in the cloakroom is still dripping and it looks bad if patients want to use it.'

'Thanks, Mick. Quite frankly, I don't know what I think of it all. I'd love to see Bea and the family in their own surroundings but I would have to leave a lot of friends if we decide to go, and Rose and Jean would miss each other.'

'Not to worry. It will all come out in the wash.'

Emma went to the kitchen smiling. 'Cup

of tea?' asked Paul and looked at her quizzically before handing her a mug. 'Did Mick have anything to say?'

'Dr Martin Allen rang up and accepted the invitation to dinner but wants to come earlier to discuss the work here.'

'Really! I invited him to dinner, not to join the firm.'

'Mick was a bit upset, as our guest seemed to think he had his feet under the table already, and Mick thought him pushy.'

'That's one valuable opinion. I suggest that we say nothing more about the appointment but listen carefully to what the others think of him, and the other candidate too, when it's his turn to eat with us. If we don't care for either, we can look again or abandon the project. People are more important than a moment of professional glory, but I really want to do this and so do you.'

'Eileen will meet them when she serves dinner and Mick will be available to give them drinks. If he's coming here about six o'clock maybe Mrs Coster would stay to open the door to him while I am busy with

Rose. Eileen and I will have to bath the children early and hope they settle quickly with no long stories read to them.' Her face clouded. 'I hate being rushed.'

'Save your opinion for later. It isn't fair to form a prejudice before you meet the man. Remember, he has no wife or child so he can't know what problems they bring! Sorry,' he said hastily. 'More tea?'

'Did you like him when you first met?'

'Yes I did. He's bright and ambitious and said that he'd already written a very good treatise on memory loss and the value of hypnosis.'

'But you want to meet him as an ordinary person and a possible friend?'

'Exactly. He'll be on his best behaviour tomorrow; good bedside manner and all the stock-in-trade of the successful shrink, and that goes for us too, I suppose, but the party is big enough to make him unwind and show his real nature if we're lucky.'

'I'll put on some music and ask what he prefers.'

'Just put on mild background music. I couldn't stand it if he opted for an evening of Wagner or pizzicato piano if that's what he likes.'

'Now who is showing his prejudices?'

'Come to bed Emma. I need to hold you and keep away the ghosts of "what if" and "perhaps it isn't wise", and tell you how much I love you.'

Three

'Having decided to do the lectures, I'll have to organise a locum soon,' Paul explained. He regarded Mick with a slight smile. 'Don't look so worried.'

'What if he wants to change things here? Bring in staff of his own? Where would that leave Eileen and me? With Sister going away with you, he might want a qualified SRN or assistant nurse to help him.'

'You know the routine and have enough experience with sterilising syringes etc. to do what is necessary. We do no surgery here so we have no theatre apparatus and techniques to concern him. Whoever comes here must understand that you are in complete charge of the office and the finances of the clinics and he will have a salary payable monthly into the bank of his choice. Eileen is officially our housekeeper and you must make sure she has a realistic amount of time off duty. Mrs Coster will come in when necessary for as many extra hours as you think you and Eileen need and you both get on well with her. Of course, he may prefer to have his own accommodation elsewhere but this place would have to be run as it is now in the interests of all of us and the patients. A lock-up consulting room and office would not do for this kind of practice. I am convinced that the warmth and pleasant atmosphere does a lot towards a patient's trust in me, and the ultimate recovery.' Paul Sykes drew some papers from the drawer. 'I have mapped out the details of your stewardship and your future salary to fit in with the extra responsibility, and Eileen's job as housekeeper must be seen to be on a regular basis.' He pushed the papers over to Mick, who read them carefully and then gave a low whistle.

'Making sure we aren't going to leave you now, aren't you, Doc? Sure you want me to take all this power?'

'We need to come back and find every-thing in order,' Paul stated. 'Also, you need to feel secure.'

Mick grinned. 'Eileen had better watch her step now and not get above herself! She'll be wanting a chain with keys round her waist.'

'She may need one if she has to lock up the larder! Dr Allen has a lean and hungry look. It's time you had your own refrigerator in your own quarters so that you are self-sufficient. Will you get that done, Mick?'

'Eileen and I can go to the Co-op tomorrow. She'll like that and she can have the divvy if that's okay with you. It mounts up and she looks on it as her perk. She's bought quite a lot with the Co-op dividend. She'll be excited as she doesn't know anyone apart from you who has a Frigidaire, but they say that nearly everyone has one in the States.'

Emma called. 'I'll start preparing for tonight while Eileen takes the children out to the local shops. Mrs Coster knows I'm going to be busy, and will open the door to patients. She says she'll be pleased to stay on to let in our guests then she'll be off to see *Me and My Girl* with her husband.'

'Gawd help us! She'll sing all day

tomorrow once she gets the hang of the tunes.' Mick sniffed. 'Well, I've a lot to do with the monthly accounts, so I'll get stuck in.'

Emma made pastry and flavoured it with cheese that had become too hard to eat in any way but grated, and cooked a mixture of diced potato, swede, carrots and sliced onions in water flavoured with two Maggi stock cubes of mushroom flavour. She thickened the vegetables with cornflour and filled a large dish lined with the pastry, covered it with more pastry and decorated it with pastry leaves. The large boiling fowl that the butcher had saved for her had been simmering in a stock made from more vegetables, bacon rind and herbs and to Emma's relief the rather adult flesh was now tender and flaking from the bones. Cut into neat pieces, the chicken, with cooked rice in a parsley sauce, would be enough for six to eight people and the pie would make it go even further.

Young pink rhubarb cooked and set in raspberry jelly would have to do for pudding, she decided, if she spared some ginger biscuits to go with it, and there was a bag of coffee beans left over from an earlier gift from Bea's father.

Paul joined her for mid-morning coffee and looked in the sideboard for drinks. 'We've enough for tonight. Grateful patients have the impression that we wallow in gin and we have two bottles of quite acceptable red wine.'

'I saved a lemon but it's a bit dried out. We can use orange concentrate for the mix. Gin and orange made with the kiddy stuff is very good and I think there is enough vermouth left if anyone prefers gin and it. Do you know? I'm quite nervous about meeting Martin Allen and I haven't even thought about the ex-naval man. He'll have to eat boiled gammon and butter beans and like it, but Mrs Coster said she can get me some spinach when her boy goes to the market, and he can buy some more carrots too. We've used our meat ration and I had to sweet talk the butcher to get a joint of ham.'

'Forget the real reason for asking Martin to dinner and enjoy a party. It could be fun.'

'Everything will be prepared in advance

and heated up, so I can join you for drinks and chat, and Eileen won't be needed to help so she can look after the children.'

Eileen brought Rose into the kitchen and gave her a cardboard box and some small patty tins to amuse her. She banged them with a wooden spoon and smiled at the sound. 'Quite musical,' Eileen announced.

'So long as no heartless friend gives her a drum for a present! Are you going to cope with two of them this evening, Eileen?'

'I'd like to bring her in to say good-night when she's ready for bed.'

Emma looked puzzled. 'You've never done that before. We look in later when she's drowsy or asleep. Fortunately she isn't a clinging child and accepts you as readily as me at bedtimes.'

'What if he doesn't like children? If the new doctor just came in for the clinic he need never see Jean or Rose, but living here, he's bound to notice and hear them. I can't keep Jean quiet all day long. I take her with me when I am working up here and she is very good at wandering out to see Mrs Coster who thinks she's lovely. Jean shouts with delight when she tickles her.'

'You must carry on as you do now, Eileen. We never find that the children interfere with serious business and they are remarkably well behaved for such tiny tots.' Emma laughed. 'Your real reason for wanting to bring Rose to say good-night is to see who my husband wants to appoint and have a good gossip about him with Mick!'

Eileen blushed. 'That too, but when I think of you going away my stomach churns and I'm frightened.'

'No, Rose!' Emma pulled her daughter from the vegetable rack and put the earthy potato back with the others. 'We'll make it as easy as we can, but Paul has to choose someone who will be efficient in the clinics and good with patients and not ruin the reputation we've built up here. If this one turns out to be really unsuitable, either professionally or as a human being, we shall think again.' She saw that Eileen had doubts. 'We have already crossed two off the list,' Emma reminded her. 'Would you rather have one bachelor who will obviously spend a lot of spare time away from the house and may not even sleep here, or a family with two large ten- and twelve-year-old boys and a big shaggy and noisy dog?'

'Crikey!' Mick said from the doorway. 'As bad as that, was it? Something smells good.' He looked serious. 'We'll have to come to terms with whatever the doc decides. He's bending over backwards to make it easy but he has a clinic to consider first. Most people wouldn't study the hired help and just push on with whatever was right for the firm.' He grinned. 'We'll manage. Now that I am really in charge of everything but the consulting room, I shall make sure that this place is run well and if necessary, I can grass on the new bloke if he is a bastard. The doc knows I'd never lie to him and he'd want my opinion.'

'Time we had something to eat, Mick. I want to tidy the dining-room this afternoon while Jean has her nap. 'I'll put out the big damask tablecloth and the serviettes, but one of them is a bit frayed so I'll slip stitch a new hem. I'll fetch Jean and take her down to our kitchen if Mrs Coster can spare her.'

'Take a jug of chicken broth,' Emma offered. 'Just thicken it, and there are lots of vegetables so it will do for Jean too.'

'What is so amusing?' Paul looked up from his diary.

'I sense a new aura of responsibility. Eileen has avoided mending linen for months but now everything has to be just right and we'll be overwhelmed by crisply starched table linen with not a hole in anything.'

'Even if we cancel our plans to go away, I think we shall gain a lot. Everyone gets into a rut at times and we can do with a shake-up. I just hope that Allen is compatible and agrees to our terms. I have consulted the British Medical Association and have their guidance about salaries for locum consultants and Beattie's unit will help if there are hitches with appointments or referrals for obstreperous patients. We have never taken patients in here but sometimes we do need access to safe beds for special cases needing restraint and supervision.'

'When do I pack?'

Paul kissed her. 'It may never happen,' he teased her. 'I think you will hate it.'

'You can't upset every one and then drop the idea now.' She held him close. 'Oh Paul, it's going to be wonderful. Imagine it. Do we go in through New York? I can't wait to see the Statue of Liberty.'

'You've been to America.'

'Only when I went with Bea in an Air Force transit plane and saw my Uncle Sydney, Emily's brother. We flew direct to an Air Force base and didn't see the statue.'

'Do you want to fly or go by liner?'

'Do we have a choice?'

'A plane would be quicker but a liner would give us more of a holiday and we could take more luggage by sea. I'll need books and papers and case histories for the lectures and you will need a lot of clothes if we are to stay away for a some while.'

'When can I tell Bea?'

'Leave it for a day or so until we have a clearer picture or she'll have a nanny lined up for you and want to arrange lots of visits to her friends.'

'A nanny? I shall look after Rose myself and feel very idle with no house to run.'

'You will need help at times. There will be

official dinners and functions where a baby would be out of place and bored, but where I shall need you to charm a lot of people. Think about it,. as our life there will take a similar course to that of Bea's. She found that a nanny was essential and I'm sure we can leave that to her.'

Emma looked uncertain for the first time. 'You may have to go away alone to be with members of university faculties and Rose and I will have to cope without you.'

'As Bea does when Dwight has official duties,' he pointed out. 'You can stay with her if I am away, and the tours are in two different groups of States, which cuts travelling down.' He grinned. 'Knowing you I have no doubt that you will fill your time and as they say over there – have a ball.'

'I shall be fat and lazy.'

Paul regarded her slim figure with approval. 'Fishing for compliments? You look wonderful, but you'll need to buy a few new clothes. They wear a lot more glitter over there and postwar England is not very bright unless you buy couture clothes like some of my wealthy patients.'

'With a small child it's too easy to dress in jumpers and skirts and low-heeled shoes, but it would be nice to dress up a little where it wouldn't look out of place.'

'Promise me you will not go with Eileen to the Co-op to buy clothes when she buys their new refrigerator.'

'I promise. I have no intention of looking like a Russian peasant. I saw Margot the other day and she looked like that. Very leftish and feminist and ready to start World War III if she could find a suitable enemy. She wouldn't approve of high fashion. The New Look made her speechless. She agreed with Mr Wilson that long skirts wasted too much cloth.'

'Wear something pretty tonight,' Paul suggested.

Emma's eyes widened. 'I suppose I could. Do I seem dowdy, Paul?'

'Never that, but you do have pretty shoes and dresses that you seem to have forgotten.'

Emma opened her wardrobe and took out an armful of clothes. She put them on the bed and examined them one by one. The ageless turquoise silk suit that Bea had exchanged for something that fitted her better at that time, looked as fresh as it had done a long time ago when she had flown to the States with Bea to see Dwight and to visit an uncle whom Emma had never met, only to find him dying of tuberculosis after a lifetime as a film actor.

'What was good enough for Uncle Sydney is certainly good enough for an aspiring psychiatrist.'

'I like it too. You had a necklace of pearls and marcasite, didn't you? I recall that you wore it with the suit.'

'Look in that box, Paul. I'd almost forgotten it.'

'It's here. Decide to wear that suit then, and come away. There isn't time for you to get dreamy over old times. Rose is calling.'

'Rose will have no problem with clothes. So many friends and clients have brought presents for her, and Bea is overwhelming with gifts as if she thinks we dress her in old potato sacks. I've reminded her that clothes rationing is over but she turns up her nose at the lack of pretty designs for children and the often skimpy finish to seams and hems.'

Paul laughed. 'Bea likes to think that she finds more exclusive garments but she still sends measurements of her twins' feet so that you can send her Clark's sandals.'

'I must make a list of what she can't get over there. They don't do everything better than we do in spite of shortages.'

'Children's feet grow fast. Stock up on several pairs of shoes to fit Rose as she gets bigger. You are going to be busy! No time to be fat and lazy,' he added with satisfaction.

Emma heard Paul greet a man and take him into the consulting room. She pursed her lips. It was earlier than she'd imagined for Martin Allen to arrive but for the moment that was Paul's problem. The last patient had left only fifteen minutes ago and Paul liked time to write up notes immediately and consider what he should do during their next appointment before other matters blurred the interview.

She bathed Rose and took her down to Eileen and Jean for a story before bedtime. The dinner was keeping hot and the drinks tray was ready, so Emma showered and changed and wondered if Paul would manage ten minutes to himself to get ready for the evening, before their other guests arrived.

Emma listened to the stranger's voice, with Paul interjecting monosyllables, and knew that she must give her husband a few minutes respite and allow him a restoring gin and orange.

'Still chatting?' she said brightly. 'I'll get Dr Allen a drink while you change, Darling.'

'But we have a lot more to discuss,' Allen said.

'We have other guests coming,' Emma said briefly. 'They will be here very soon and Paul needs to get ready. It's time you both forgot work for a while,' she added sweetly. 'I hope you like the others. They are pleasant and humorous and we're looking forward to a good social evening.'

'See you later,' Paul said, and escaped.

Dr Allen watched him go with a hint of resentment but Emma led him firmly into the sitting-room. She handed him a drink and motioned towards a comfortable chair.

'Are the others who are coming tonight candidates for the post?' he asked after sipping his drink and trying to look relaxed.

'No. We try not to mix business with entertaining. Paul likes to give his full attention to each situation and was rather surprised that you wanted to come here before the time we expected you for dinner, just to talk shop.' She eyed him seriously. 'I think you've both talked of that enough, in what should be leisure time. The others would be bored stiff to have to listen to accounts of other people's obsessions and paranoia, as they are not medics, except for the Sister I invited from Beatties who will want to talk of anything but work.'

'I want to come here and I know I can do the work.'

'You wouldn't have been given an invitation to apply for it if Paul thought he was wasting his time and yours, but he is just compiling a shortlist and we aren't in a hurry to leave until we are certain we are ready.'

'Some people think I'm brash and pushy. You don't think that, do you? It's just that I am anxious to get on and have to get in before the opposition.'

Emma was saved from replying. Rose was laughing and trying to run away from Eileen to hug Catharine, who was one of her favourite people. Dr Allen stared as the child rushed into the sitting-room and flung herself onto a low stool. She was pink-cheeked and tendrils of curling hair fringed her face. Emma smiled tenderly and glanced at Allen to see his reaction to the lovely child but he seemed unmoved.

'Come here!' Eileen grabbed Rose and held her high in her arms. 'Say good-night and God bless and then it's time for bed.' Emma kissed Rose and Eileen turned away towards the door as there was no sign that Dr Allen wanted to speak to Rose or for her to look at him. The door closed behind Eileen and the others, who went out to take off their outdoor clothes.

'She'll go with you to America?' Dr Allen asked hopefully.

Emma half smiled. 'Of course, but Jean, who is about the same age and belongs to our housekeeper, will be here to liven the place up. This house isn't just part of the business, this is home to two families.'

He looked puzzled. 'How does that fit into a psychiatric clinic?'

'Paul believes that patients who are disturbed need to feel comfortable in their surroundings. He never lets our family life interfere with clinics, but when patients need just to talk of everyday matters, we give them tea and biscuits and perhaps more of our private time than is usual.' Dr Allen seemed doubtful. 'It works,' Emma said briefly. 'I think the others are all here now, so would you mix a jug of gin and orange. I've diluted the orange as it comes in a thick syrup, but it's really very good.' She laughed. 'We have more gin than suitable mixers and lemons are still difficult to buy.'

Catharine took Emma to one side. 'I wanted to bring something but the off-licence had only that awful British sherry that you don't like so I brought something above the price of rubies!'

Emma took the paper bag, tied up with an incongruous bow of blue ribbon and opened it. 'Bananas? Can you really spare them? I managed to have some about two months ago and I haven't seen any since. Oranges are more plentiful now, but bananas! The babies will love them mashed with custard.'

'A friend came off a boat from the West Indies and brought a lot of fruit with him. Some were a bit over ripe by the time he got home, but most were edible and there were fruits that I had never seen, like mangoes. He bought unripe bananas, so they travelled well and would you believe, my darling daughter who had never seen one, tried to eat it skin and all when I handed one to her to look at before I skinned it for her.'

'Did she enjoy it?'

'I was glad I gave her a small piece to try. Ungrateful child spat it out and refused any more, so we ate the rest when she was in bed.'

'Do you remember that during the war a doctor appealed on the wireless for anyone who had bananas brought home by soldiers and sailors on leave should hand them in to feed children with coeliac disease?'

'What's that?'

'Babies are born with a digestive problem. They can't eat anything with wheat in it, and when you think about it there wasn't a lot of food that had no bread in it in wartime. In Holland, after the Germans took all the wheat harvests to Germany and left the Dutch starving and trying to use potatoes and even flower bulbs to make up for wheat, they found that the coeliac babies no longer died, but thrived, so they discovered something useful through what was for most people a tragedy.'

Emma thought of George, her naval officer cousin who had a talent for bringing back otherwise unobtainable presents such as bananas and oranges from abroad ... Dear kind George who had been in love with her and who deserved to find happiness and make a home for the small son left to him after his wife Sadie died of meningitis.

'I hope Dr Allen's made the drinks strong enough,' Emma said. 'I think there's a streak of the puritan in our maybe new doctor.'

'Or plain selfishness?' suggested Catharine.

'This is the first time I've met him,' Emma replied.

'Me too, but he isn't as nice as Paul.'

'Who is?'

'I would never feel that I could tell Dr Allen about my hang-ups and I doubt if he'd understand.'

'Let's see how we feel about him after this evening,' Emma suggested. 'I wanted you two here tonight as we can use a few unbiased opinions. You are coming to dinner again if you can bear it the day after tomorrow, to do the same when we have our ex-naval type for an evening.'

'I can hardly wait. I love being nosy.'

Four

'If he comes here, he'll want to be waited on hand and foot,' Mick warned his wife.

'He's very good-looking and he enjoyed his dinner,' Eileen said. 'He was ever so interested in where he'd sleep and things like that, as if he knew he'd be coming here.'

'Maybe,' Mick said cryptically. 'I want to see who else the doc has lined up.'

'You didn't like him.'

'If the doc says he comes here, then I'll put up with it but I can't say I'd be thrilled to have him about the place all the time.'

'I'd rather he slept out,' Eileen agreed, with conviction.

'Now who doesn't like him? I thought you lapped up the nice things he said about the way the house was cared for, and wanted to know if you'd be cooking his meals,' Mick said dryly.

'I wouldn't want someone who didn't

enjoy his food.' Eileen sounded defensive.

'He'd want to know all that, but mark my words, he's all for number one. I bet he works by the book and would finish with a patient so that he could have his dinner. Doc never does that and sometimes he misses a meal if he thinks the patient needs more time.'

'He had his eyes on the bananas they brought, and I think he'd have pinched one if I hadn't taken them down to our kitchen. Cheek! I told him that they were for the children and he said he hadn't had a banana for ages and really liked them. "What the children haven't had they'll never miss," he said, so I told him that goes for us too, and him! You like banana custard but you won't have any until we can buy them easily. We had some once when a pal of yours came home on leave, do you remember? That was before Jean was born so we made pigs of ourselves over them and didn't have to share with anyone, but now Jean comes first and we wouldn't dream of touching anything that would do her good.'

Emma, who had come into the kitchen,

caught the last of the conversation. She handed Mick the list of goods they needed to replenish stocks of food ready for the next dinner party. He thought that he might be lucky enough to find some things in the street market. 'I'd hoped the shortages were lessening, even so, we can't get some things unless we queue for them,' she said. 'See what's available and I'll use whatever you order. I need cooking fat today. That pie was good. I'll make another like it as it goes with most dishes and will help out the gammon. My cousin George kept Aunt Janey supplied with bananas for a time and she sent me some but he gave the next lot to the hospitals when he heard that babies were dying of a wasting disease because they couldn't absorb gluten in wheat. He made sure his men gave up the fruit they brought home, too.'

'Now he's what I call a really nice man.'

'You've seen him only once or twice, Eileen.' Emma told her.

'He made me laugh and was ever so friendly.'

'Yes, he's a good man,' Emma said slowly.

'I hope he gets married soon and Clive has a happy home with his new mother. My Aunt Janey says she's lovely and very fond of Clive.'

'Will you be here for the wedding?'

'I doubt it,' Emma replied lightly. 'We may be in America if we have found someone to take over the clinics. I have to go to see Luigi and Mario in the restaurant.' She went into the consulting room. 'Do you need me?' she asked her husband.

Paul frowned. 'We have half an hour before the next session and I've been thinking about one or two snags. Having Allen here made a lot of things clear. I have no intention of anyone taking over my private clinic, although he seemed to think that he would manage. I stressed that the appointed locum would be salaried and would cope only with the National Health Service list and emergencies. He was put out and said I must learn to trust him.'

'That was a bit of a nerve.'

'I've already mentioned to Shilton that I'd like him to follow up any private patients who need help so they would see him at his home and not come here. In fact, the workload here won't be excessive. Just the general patients according to my Health Service contract and emergencies. For a start, Allen hasn't done any hypnosis and isn't as well qualified as I'd been told. Analysis is about his level and any neurological disorders he finds should be referred to Beatties or St Thomas'. He's more a psychotherapist than a psychiatrist or neurologist as yet and the danger would be that he might think himself more clever than he is and try to be too adventurous.' Paul looked pensive. 'I picked up more than he seems to know just by watching Shilton and a few others, and yet he gives the impression that he knows it all, which I distrust. On paper he has an impressive list of names with whom he worked in Edinburgh.'

'Why not pass all the work over to Dr Shilton and start up again after we return?'

'I need continuity here and must provide a locum for the National Health clinics. Even if we engage someone to live out and come in for set sessions, Mick will have a lot of paperwork to do and Eileen will have to provide meals and keep the consulting room clean and efficiently run. That will take a lot of time when you aren't here.'

'We'll see what the other doctor is like this evening. I know that Eileen is anxious to see him. Mick is resilient and has had to deal with all kinds of people but Eileen would be thoroughly miserable with an unsympathetic doctor here. Looking back to the time when we first employed them, Eileen was very withdrawn and a bit helpless, as she has never trained for anything. Full marks to her and to the safety she feels living here and being married to a strong character like Mick. It has allowed her to be more assertive, but I could see that she was very worried when Dr Allen took no notice when she brought Rose in to say good-night, as if Eileen and children were of no importance and could be ignored as a necessary evil.'

'He made a point of talking to her later when she brought in coffee,' Paul conceded.

'He was anxious to find out if he would be well looked after!'

Paul shrugged. 'No decisions until tomorrow. I'm fairly sure that Martin Allen isn't who we want and if I'm not satisfied with Commander Forsyth, we try again.'

Mick called through on the intercom. 'Call for you, Doc. Dr Allen wants a word.'

'Tell him that I am busy and have patients to see all day. He can leave a message if he has anything to add to what we talked about last night but I shall not be in touch with him until I have interviewed everyone on my shortlist.'

'Fair enough, Doc.' Mick sounded pleased.

'He'll enjoy telling Dr Allen that he must not ring again,' Emma said. 'What do you need for the next patient?'

'Not even a chaperone. Why not take Rose to the park for an hour? It's a lovely morning.'

'I'll take the pushchair and her reins. When Eileen or I take both the children it's wise to strap them into the big twin pram that Bea left us as they are so active. I can manage one if I take reins to stop Rose darting away and the pushchair is handy if she gets tired. See you for lunch.'

'There's a pretty girl,' Mrs Coster said as Emma pulled the pushchair from the hall cupboard. 'It's warm out there now and the grass is dry. Have a nice walk.' She swept Rose up in a firm hug and kissed her cheek.

'Bye,' Rose said and waved as Emma led her out through the doorway.

'Don't let her learn too much American,' Mrs Coster said and shook her head. 'I don't know why you want to go away. It will be very dull without you, and little Jean will feel it very much.'

'We haven't decided when we are going,' Emma reminded her, and left before Mrs Coster could go into details about the terrible things that happened in New York. She knew it was all true as she'd seen it in the cinema.

The air was warm, and fresh green softened the gaunt trees. Soon there would be no clear view across the park when the leaves burgeoned and shaded the paths. Rose made a rumbling sound with her lips as the pushchair went over the rough side path, then wanted to walk when there was no sound from the wheels and they joined the well-paved lane to the statue of Peter Pan. Rose laughed with delight and struggled against the reins that Emma insisted that she wore to restrain her if she suddenly saw something exciting and tried to investigate.

'We'll take a picture of Peter Pan to Aunt Bea when we go to America.' Emma said almost to herself.

'Bea-Bea,' Rose said and chuckled. 'Peter.'

The statue was badly marked with pigeon droppings but the carved animals were enough to satisfy a small child and Rose was, as always, fascinated by the monument to eternal youth. They walked until Rose demanded to sit in the pushchair and Emma took her to the row of local shops that had sprung up at the end of the war and now seemed as if they had been there forever. Mario, Luigi's father, brought out two bottles of wine that Paul had asked him to save if there were enough to spare from the restaurant and Rose graciously accepted a biscuit covered with hard white icing.

'When you give her a little brother?' he asked as usual. 'Maybe not yet until you come back from America? You don't want him to be American.' He tapped his very Italian chest. 'You want him to be British like me.'

'I'll think about it, but just now all I can manage is another dinner party for a colleague of Paul's.'

'Maybe he will not find a good man and you will stay?' He asked hopefully, and Emma felt a surge of misgiving. What if there was no likely candidate? She realised just how much she wanted to go to America and she hurried back, willing the ex-naval officer to be right for the clinic and for the house she loved.

'Do you want me here when the doctor arrives?' Mrs Coster asked.

'No, I think he is coming at the appointed time for the dinner party and not earlier to talk about work with my husband first. Eileen can put the girls to bed and we can meet our guests when they arrive. Don't look so disappointed. Eileen will no doubt tell you all about him, and if he comes to work here you'll see enough of him later.'

Mrs Coster looked at her employer and

then away. 'I was saying to my Maureen ... no, it's none of my business.'

'What were you saying?' Emma asked politely, knowing that Mrs Coster had every intention of speaking her mind.

'Well, the truth is that I said I didn't care for the doctor who came here and I can't see him getting on with the patients we have here.'

'He is qualified as a doctor but hasn't a lot of experience of neurological conditions or psychiatry, or not as much as we had hoped, but he's very keen to come here.'

Mrs Coster sniffed. 'He wanted to know who would do his laundry.'

'Not you, and we haven't appointed him or anyone. We have to see at least one more doctor, and probably we may advertise.'

'Did he do his training in London? I can't see him as a Beatties man. All my family go to Beatties and I know a doctor from there a mile off.'

Emma frowned. 'I think he trained in Ireland but when Sister Bright asked him, he changed the subject and said that Paul didn't want him to talk shop. That was after he'd been trying to do just that all through the first course!'

Mrs Coster looked complacent. 'What did I tell you? He isn't one of ours.'

'You look a bit pensive,' Paul remarked, meeting his wife at the doorway of his office.

'Mrs Coster seems to think that Dr Allen is less than human because he didn't train in London. I told her that other medical schools did wonderful work and had world-wide reputations but she sniffed in the way she does when something smells bad or doesn't come up to standard.'

'I must telephone Shilton and ask if he knows of Allen.'

'Does he worry you as much as that?'

'It's being surrounded by suspicious women that makes me anxious! Or I hope it is.' He sat down at his desk. 'Was that call for me?' he asked Mick who was sorting the mail.

'Someone checking the time of an appointment. All okay, Doc.'

Emma followed Mick to the kitchen where Eileen was making pancakes for lunch. She heard Eileen giggle and the couple stopped

84

talking when she came past them to fetch a drink for Rose.

'Who rang, Mick?' she asked. Mick turned on the tap and filled a tumbler with water, drank it and made for the door. *'Mick!'*

'It was Dr Allen again, Sister.' Mick looked suspiciously innocent. 'The doc told me he didn't want to speak to him again until he's seen some more possible shrinks.'

'So what did he want?'

'He asked when Commander Forsyth was coming to dinner as he met him at the conference and wanted to meet him again. He said he could meet him here for a chat; as if he owned the place,' Mick added.

'That's not his business! And this isn't a social club.'

'That's what I thought, Sister, and I didn't want to worry the doc,' Mick said virtuously.

'So what did you tell him?' Emma distrusted the self-imposed halo and waited for Mick to reply truthfully.

'I said the Commander was coming here tomorrow.'

'Oh dear, I thought we were having a party

85

tonight.' Emma laughed. 'Why did you tell him the wrong night?'

'Don't want him walking in on us tonight, do we? Might want another meal and a good look at the opposition. And he tries to pick the doc's brains as if he knows very little himself; but as he thinks he's one of the anointed he thinks he can take liberties.'

'That's ridiculous,' Emma replied but could think of no other reason for Dr Allen's curiosity.

Mick grinned. 'Better have baked beans on toast tomorrow for supper or fish cakes from Lyons.'

'I don't like fish cakes,' Emma replied, then smiled. 'If he smelled the gammon boiling, he'd have his table napkin under his chin before anyone. I did find him pushy,' she admitted.

'It's not just that he wants to be fed and have a comfortable billet. That is what we all want but I hope the doc has checked his qualifications.'

'What do you mean?'

'I've been here long enough to have memorised a lot of what is said and done in there.' Mick looked serious. 'At a pinch I could talk to patients as the doc does and know what I was talking about.' He grinned. 'Maybe I'll set up on my own. It's wonderful what you can pick up from just listening and from books.'

'That's ridiculous. You may be a genius Mick, but some things must be beyond even you.'

'That sex-mad woman and psychotics would be.'

'Glad to hear it,' Eileen said primly.

'The butter beans have soaked all night and I've put them in the oven on a very low heat,' Emma said. 'We can cook the spinach at the last minute and I think the carrots would be good mashed with a little orange juice.'

'I can see I'm not wanted,' Mick said.

'Have your lunch, Eileen. I'll see if Paul has finished with the last patient. I think I have time to take some polish into the office as there is a dark patch where a vase overflowed by the bookcase.'

The smell of wax polish was friendly and reminded Emma of the days long ago when the pupil probationers in the Home on the Bristol Downs had to polish the rows of leather cases stored in the luggage room that was a haven for junior nurses, where they could escape the rasping tongue of Sister Cary. She rubbed the patch until the dullness disappeared, then noticed some dust inside the glass doors of the large book cupboard. She looked again and saw that there were gaps among the books. Two large books on psychoanalysis and one on schizophrenia were missing.

Emma looked into the consulting room and saw that Paul was alone. 'Lunch is ready when you are free,' she said. 'I didn't know that you were selecting books for America. I suppose we have to take some but those ones are very heavy.'

'Which ones?'

'Two on basic analysis and one on delusions.'

Paul looked into the bookcase. 'I haven't touched them for ages. Those are fairly basic and I don't need them now. I was considering putting them into the medical library at Beatties but it seems that someone got here first,' he added dryly.

'Mick often reads medical books but he reads them here and puts them back,' Emma assured him.

'I was thinking of our visitor. After the dinner party, he made an excuse to come back to the office to fetch the briefcase he left here and then hurried out.'

'He worried you?'

'I've been telephoning a few people. Nobody remembers who brought him to the congress or knows where he trained, but Maurice thought he knew the name from Dublin. He said he'd find out more and ring back.'

'Did you think he was well qualified to take clinics?'

'No, and until I know more about him I shall not encourage him. I wish I'd not invited him here but it was awkward. I invited George's friend for a purely social evening and at that time, the possibility of a locum had been mentioned only in passing. I said nothing about interviews. Allen on the other hand took it that I wanted to see both men as possible candidates and was hurt that I gave an advantage to a friend of a friend.' Paul shrugged. 'The dinner was a success and I hope you enjoyed it but he pressured me and wanted to sit in with me on some cases almost as if he was a student.'

Emma hesitated. 'He rang again today.'

'The hell he did!'

'He wanted to know when Commander Forsyth was coming here as he wanted to meet him again to discuss a couple of things.'

'Did you speak to him?'

'No need. Your steward takes his duties seriously. He told Dr Martin Allen that we are entertaining the Commander tomorrow, but said nothing of them meeting here.'

'Tomorrow? They are coming today.'

'Exactly. Mick suggested that we have fish cakes for supper tomorrow when we are alone in case he arrives expecting to be fed!'

'Good old Mick. The effrontery of the man amuses me, but this could be serious. I see a lot of innocent-looking charmers in there and they are often the worst kind of con men.'

Mick poked his head round the doorway

and raised an eyebrow. 'A Dr Maurice Flynn is on the phone.'

'It's okay, Mick. I am expecting this call.'

'Did you tell him the other one called, Sister?'

'Yes and he approves of what you said.'

'Thank Gawd for that.'

'Paul?' the caller enquired.

'Speaking.'

'I spoke to a friend.' There was silence for a few moments and Maurice Flynn coughed.

'Tell me, Maurice. I have grave suspicions about Allen and need to know the worst.'

'He was a medical student in Dublin, fluffed his exams and wangled a course in Edinburgh by pleading ill health after being bombed as a youth during the war. He was no good and it is rumoured that he stole money and books from other students, but he escaped prosecution. They were glad to see the back of him, so pressed no charges. Since then he has been a medical orderly and came south where nobody knew him.'

'Thank you very much. I have a feeling that this is serious from several points of view. Not only is he passing himself off as a fully qualified medic but he has grandiose ideas that he can safely treat psychiatric patients.'

'You have to alert the police, Paul. He is a menace and a criminal and I think in need of treatment in an institution. I've sent you an account of his history and you can pass it on to the authorities.'

'I'll be in touch, and thank you, Maurice' Paul replied soberly. 'I hate to do this but I think he's ill and must be stopped before he does harm.' He replaced the receiver, deep in thought.

'Everything all right, Doc?'

'No.' Paul told Emma and Mick of the telephone conversation.

'You'll have to wait until Dr Flynn's letter arrives, possibly tomorrow morning, with documentary evidence, so you can't go to the police today,' Mick said firmly. 'He can't do much harm for a day or so but if the letter arrives tomorrow, we know where he'll be tomorrow evening. I know a bloke at the local police station. I'll go round tomorrow. If they want to arrest him they can pick him up before he comes here. At least we know his address.'

Emma bit her lip. This was so like the time when Bea had to report a German officer who thought she couldn't understand German and said obscene things to her in the ward of German prisoners of war. It was all said with a broad friendly smile. The other prisoners laughed and showed signs of being difficult. The military police took him from the ward as soon as they knew and the other men in the ward were very well behaved after he had gone. The military policeman had reassured Bea when she said she felt guilty, that she had been sensible to report him. He said that one rotten apple in a barrel destroyed the good fruit and the men would be very co-operative in the future.

'I hate this,' Emma said, 'But I know it has to happen. What will they do to Dr Allen?'

'As soon as they have proof that he is posing as a doctor and is a fraud, he will be treated – but not by me,' Paul reassured her.

'Let's hope the Navy is okay.' Mick grinned. 'I have a better feeling about this evening.'

Five

'Is this a bad time to call?' asked Emily Darwen anxiously.

'No, Aunt Emily. We do have people coming to dinner in half an hour but everything is ready and Eileen is seeing to the drinks tray.'

Emma told her who had been invited and when she mentioned Commander Forsyth, Emily said, 'That's a friend of George. He was in the Navy with him but now he's Dr Forsyth. George told me all about him. He was a very good naval officer, but took the offer the government made to officers in the services, to go to university when they left for civilian life. Robert's ambition was to be a doctor.'

'You've met him?'

'When he was in Portsmouth after he had come out of the Navy and had his medical degree. George stayed with him for a weekend and brought him over to the island. That seems a long time ago but I'd like to meet him again. I gave them a meal. You'll like him,' she said firmly as if Emma would not dare to doubt her opinion.

'It's good to have an unbiased testimonial,' Emma said dryly.

'I suppose he ate everything in sight and drank your strong whisky tea after the meal.'

'Of course he did, but apart from that, George said that he is a very good doctor and is now involved in the same work as Paul.'

'How is George?'

'Janey is very happy about the future for him and I can't see much wrong either. Just you keep away until he's settled into marriage and he'll be fine.'

'We shall be in America when he is married.'

'Good girl.'

'You want to get rid of me!'

'For a while. Bea needs you and I think you need her, and Paul has work to do, so go now and enjoy America, then come to stay and bring my great-niece to see me.'

'Give George my love.'

'I'll do no such thing. I'll say you rang and that Rose and Paul are well. George will always love you, Emma, but he will be happy. His fiancee was engaged to be married but he was drowned in the Pacific, so she and George have every chance of understanding each other. Personal tragedy for both of them must smooth off a few rough edges and make them softer, unless they go the other way and close up. I think they are strong enough to make a good life together. They'll be fine,' she added.

Emma told Emily about Martin Allen and was amused when Emily promised to write a testimonial for Robert Forsyth to make sure he became Paul's locum.

'You've fallen for him.'

'I like a nicely set up young man,' Emily replied coolly. 'I may be an old woman but I still know an attractive and good man when I see one.'

'That gives me courage. I was dreading Paul having to advertise and see lots of strange people coming here to be interviewed.'

'Are you going by ship?'

'We've made no plans but I've never been on a liner. Paul needs a holiday before he starts his lecture tours so a few days being pampered would be lovely.'

'I'd rather you went by sea.'

'Why?'

'Just a feeling. I can wave as you pass down Southampton Water. I spent a day at Cowes with Clive. He knows all the shapes of the big liners and adores the sea. Give my love to Rose and Paul and get back to the kitchen. What's for dinner?' Emma told her and Emily approved. 'I've a bush of parsley that needs picking. It would have gone well with butter beans to make parsley sauce. Wilf sowed it in the conservatory and I have it all through the year now.'

Joan Bright arrived and was very curious to hear about Martin Allen. 'We had no time to chat after dinner but have you heard anything from him? I wangled another evening off as I just couldn't miss seeing the next man on your list. I hope that Paul has gone off the idea of taking Martin into the practice?'

'Paul never had that idea. It was Martin Allen who tried to make Paul see him as the only one for the post, but he will be lucky not to be arrested.'

'Real trouble? I'm not surprised. I caught him out on one or two clinical things when he was rabbiting on about what he had done and who he had worked with.'

'He's not qualified as a doctor, even after two attempts. He had a doubtful reputation in Edinburgh as a student and he was a medical orderly before he came south.'

'He must have read a lot to think he could cope with psychiatry.'

'So I believe and he does have a great opinion of himself. He walked off with two or three of Paul's books without mentioning them, so I can't see him bringing them back. Paul thinks he needs treatment and may be schizoid. Whatever he is, he isn't fit to be released onto the public as a shrink.'

'There's a grey area here,' Sister Bright said. 'If he claimed to be a qualified doctor, he is in trouble for that, but if he just says he practises psychoanalysis, he may get away with it, as anyone can say he is a psychologist. Aren't we all? We need to be, to deal with some of the devious characters in the wards or who come to Casualty hoping to get a bed for the night on the strength of an imagined ailment.' Joan laughed. 'We sort out a lot of them by producing a large tray of instruments, which I must say are never used, and a large syringe which we say we need to take blood for tests. The Casualty technician asks if the patient needs to strip completely for the examination, and surprise!, the condition is suddenly non-existent and the cubicle is empty as soon as my back is turned.'

'What if you miss genuine cases?'

'I don't think we do. They stay and are eager to be helped. I'm sure you have ideas about who is a sham?'

'I do, and so do most nurses and doctors. It didn't take any of us long before we labelled Martin as an attractive fraud, but Paul did a lot of careful checking.' Emma smiled. 'It was hardly necessary. Mrs Coster, our cleaner, didn't like him, Mick and Eileen hoped he would not come here again and you decided that he wasn't genuine. Go into the drawing-room while I bring the others up for drinks.'

The handshake was warm and firm, the eyes glinted with humour and the mouth was as Bea would say, just full enough for interest and not too outrageous to be a threat.

'It's good to meet you at last,' Robert Forsyth said. 'I've heard a lot about you from George.'

'I've just been speaking to my Aunt Emily and she asked to be remembered to you,' Emma said demurely, avoiding any reference to her cousin. 'Come and meet the others. Paul will be here as soon as he's finished in the office.'

If he was Martin Allen, he'd have been in the office after Paul, eager for what he could learn of the practice and making Paul late to meet the other guests, Emma thought, and sighed with relief.

'I loved it there when George took me to lunch with her. She's a very good cook.' He laughed. 'I'm glad she liked me. I had the impression that if I fell short of her high standards she'd give me no pudding.'

'Did she make you drink that awful tea with lots of whisky in it?'

He shuddered in mock alarm. 'That habit doesn't run in the family, does it? I was glad not to be driving that day and I had a terrible hangover, but I could forgive her everything for that wonderful apple pie. Do you think she'd invite me again?'

'I'm sure she would.' Emma's lips twitched. 'She said you looked more like a sailor than a doctor and being an islander, she likes sailors.'

'I heard that not all islanders feel the same,' he said, solemnly. 'By the way, George is very well.'

'I know. It's wonderful that he is engaged. Clive needs a full family life.' He gave her a keen look and nodded approval and she knew that he could delve into minds as Paul did, gently and relentlessly, until the patients involved told the truth and eased their minds in a process of self-healing.

'What a lovely house. It must make a lot of difference to patients to come in here and be surrounded by what is so obviously a friendly and comfortable home.'

Emma smiled. 'Sometimes too comfortable, and they try to persuade Paul that they need treatment here for a couple of weeks, but we never take residential cases.'

'Very wise.'

Joan Bright handed Robert a drink and gave a thumbs up sign to Emma when his back was turned to greet the other guests. 'All right, just don't eat him before dinner,' Emma whispered.

'I thought I'd pop up to see if you wanted any help.' Eileen said, appearing at Emma's side and taking in every detail of the doctor, from his well-polished shoes to his silk paisley tie and shining hair. 'Mick is downstairs so he can keep an eye on Jean. She's not settling and I think she has another tooth coming through.'

'You've seen him now – satisfied?' Emma teased. 'Oh dear! I think your door is on the latch again. Someone has escaped.'

'You little devil,' Eileen said as Jean waddled in, wearing a bright pink winceyette nightdress and trailing her small 'comfort' blanket.

Robert saw her and laughed. 'You look like

my brother's infant.' He bent down and smoothed her reddened cheek. 'Where's your teething ring?'

Eileen was enchanted. She brought a large silver spoon which Jean seized and rubbed against her inflamed gums, beaming up at the kind face that gave her confidence, just as her father's did.

Eileen picked her up and carried her downstairs where Mick stood by the door to their apartment. 'You'll have to get that door fixed,' she said accusingly.

'I did it yesterday but I knew she'd want to have a look at the new man so all I did was to shoo her upstairs and say go and find Mummy, and she thought it was fun.'

'Oh, you are awful, Mick Grade!'

'Well what did you think?'

'Nice! He has good hands and is ever so nice-looking.'

'Right! That settles it. We can't have him here if he's going to make you all of a tizzy!'

'Then why do you look so smug?'

'I asked if I could put his car away when I happened to see him from the front porch, and he was pleased, as he didn't want it left on the road. He looked up at the house and grinned at me. 'Posh aren't you?' he said. Reminded me of my old CO. No side and lots of laughs with him even when he was telling you off. Never said a word unless you deserved it and then you never felt put down, if you know what I mean? But whatever it was you did wrong, you never did again. You can tell he's used to Navy discipline.'

'You were Army, Mick.'

'Same thing really. A good'un never loses it.'

'Sailors are tidy. Not like that other one would have been.'

'Doc might not decide on him, or Sister might not want a friend of her George here. What if he asked him to stay?'

'When he's married it won't matter and the family will be away, silly.'

'Jean's getting drowsy. I'll put her in her cot if you make the tea. What's for our supper?'

'Mrs Coster's Alfie got a pint of shrimps for us and some crab claws so we can have a treat. I made some bread for us when I made it for Sister upstairs and it's nice and fresh.'

Mick came back into the room after settling his daughter and raised his beer. 'Cheers. I have a feeling that once again Mick and Eileen Grade are going to land on their feet. If our Jean likes him and you do, we are halfway home.'

'Mrs Coster will want to hear all about him. She was dying to stay tonight to see him arrive.'

'Tomorrow will be soon enough for her and tomorrow night I'd better be around in case there's trouble, unless Mr Allen has been warned off or picked up by the law.'

'He wasn't really bad. He was polite and he wanted to come here,' Eileen began.

'Look at you! Making excuses for him. Just like you to be brought round by a few sweet words. He knew he could charm anyone if he tried long enough, but not Sister, that's for sure.'

'Dr Forsyth met Sister's Aunt Emily,' Eileen said with deep meaning.

'If *she* approved then we needn't worry about him,' Mick replied. 'Come on, Girl, let's do the washing up and listen to the wireless.'

Paul ground the precious coffee beans and put them to steep in a large earthenware jug of boiling water and Emma set out a plate of biscuits on the sitting-room table. The aroma of good coffee by the wood fire made Joan Bright sigh.

'This is like home used to be,' she said. 'I remember that smell in my grannie's kitchen and cried when they told me that she had been bombed out and it was all gone.'

Emma felt nostalgic too but not for family comfort. Her memory was of a small instrument steriliser bubbling gently, with a jug of coffee simmering and ready for theatre staff and surgeons to drink after the cases were done, or when visitors came to brighten the long night-duty hours when the ward on which she was working was slack. 'It's good to have the excuse to use the good coffee beans,' she said when Robert remarked on the flavour. 'It takes me back.'

'I think I told more personal secrets to

near strangers over cups of steriliser brew than I'd dream of confessing to another living soul,' Joan Bright said. 'With so many different medics coming to Beatties and Heath Cross in Surrey, we saw a lot of new faces and most of them felt fed up, far from home and ready to talk to anyone who would listen.'

'So you gave what the textbooks never tell us, essential tea and sympathy and friendship?'

She looked at Robert sharply. 'All that at times and it was difficult to remain professionally aloof when they were a little ... overwhelmed.'

He smiled. 'I doubt if you knew just what an impact you all made on medical students, and patients who were suffering but were emotionally mature men.'

Emma giggled. 'We had our moments and at times had to take avoiding action. It was convenient to have both Beatties and Heath Cross hospitals, as our friends could say we had been transferred to the other one if an ex-patient was too pushy and tried to contact us after they'd been discharged.'

'I had letters.' Joan smiled. 'Some were pathetic but it wasn't a good thing to reply. More seriously, some were the moral blackmail sort ... If you won't see me I'll kill myself.'

'What did you do about them?' Catharine was fascinated as the only time she'd been in hospital was when she had had her tonsils removed as a child.

'We handed over the letters to Admin if we were alarmed and they referred them to their own doctors. We heard no more from them.'

'So you emerged unscathed?' Robert regarded her with more interest than might be expected during a casual dinner party date.

'Pretty well,' Joan said enigmatically and refused to meet his gaze. She looked at the ormolu clock on the mantelpiece, a gift from Emily Darwen brought from the house on the Mall where Emma's grandmother had lived. 'I'll have to go,' she said. 'Is that the right time? That's a lovely clock.'

'My aunt had it cleaned and overhauled with a few other nice pieces that my grandmother left and it keeps perfect time.'

'It *is* late,' Robert agreed. He stood and gave one last look at the glowing fire. 'No wonder your patients want to stay here.' He handed Joan her small evening bag. 'Come along. I can see you safely home.' Emma gave Catharine a warning glance. After the last dinner, she and her husband had driven Joan back to Beatties. Catharine smiled and sat back again, and Paul rang for Mick to bring Robert's car from the garage.

'More coffee, Catharine?' Emma asked.

'We haven't talked shop,' Paul said as Robert followed him with Emma to fetch his coat. 'I'd like to see you again as soon as possible.' He raised an eyebrow in a silent question and the two men smiled.

'Come again soon,' Emma added. 'After all, before Paul asks you to join us we must see what our very perceptive Mrs Coster thinks of you.' Her eyes sparkled. 'Mick and Eileen have given you the all clear, especially as you seem to like children, so come to coffee tomorrow if you have the time.'

'What about other candidates? You must

have a shortlist of very well-qualified men.'

'If you find us bearable, we'd like you to come,' Paul affirmed.

'Thank you,' Robert said simply.

'I'll ring you tomorrow, Emma,' Joan said then whispered, 'Do you think he'll want a part-time Sister? I could fit him in during my spells off duty.'

'Hush! He'll read your mind. In that respect, he's rather like Paul.'

'Nice car,' Mick said after the guests had all departed and Emma had offered him some coffee. 'Is he coming here, Doc?'

'I hope so. He's very bright and has the right manner for this work.'

'Where is he living now?' Emma wanted to know.

'He has a small flat near Covent Garden which he will keep as a permanent base and live here for some of the time. He needs to be further into town for some things but wants to use a room here when he is busy. I don't think he'll be too much for you and Eileen to cope with.'

'He mentioned a married brother who has a small child. Is Robert ... attached?'

'There's hope for Joan Bright yet,' Paul said dryly.

'They got on very well,' Emma agreed.

'I'll tell Eileen the good news. She can't sleep until she hears the gossip. Good-night all.' Mick took his leave.

'Let's sit by the fire. It's still warm in there,' Emma said. She looked amused. 'Do we employ Eileen and Mick or do they rule us?'

'Neither. We have an arrangement and a mutual respect. We are so lucky.'

Emma snuggled into Paul's arms. 'So very lucky.'

'Tomorrow you can ring Bea and say that we have definite plans to visit them if they can suggest a simple bed and breakfast place.'

'That will send her tearing about finding somewhere like the White House for us if she doesn't completely disrupt their own home just for three extra bods.'

'I expect that Emily will know by now, so there is no need to ring *her* to tell her,' Paul teased her.

'I'll have to go down to the island before

we go away. Emily has several pieces of crochet that she's made for Bea. The Americans go mad over them and she could sell them for a lot of money but she likes to give them away to Bea and me and a few chosen friends.'

'We must take them presents. What can't they get over there?'

'Not much, but Wilf makes wooden toys that are rather good and if we go by boat, we can take a lot of things that we couldn't manage by air.'

'A few rolls of films are a good idea. Bea loves London and we can take snaps of improvements made since she left England.

'I wanted Wilf to make a rocking horse for Rose. If he started it now it would be ready for her in a year's time, but Aunt Emily was against the idea, so I didn't suggest that he made one for Bea's twins.'

'Why was that? I had one when I was very young and loved it. Maybe we should have one in the consulting room for patients who had been deprived of rocking horses in childhood.' He laughed. 'The action is very soothing and nearly everyone loves them.'

'When I asked what she had against the idea, Aunt Emily told me about a child in the family who had been nearly killed when she fell off a wooden horse. I believe she was disabled for a long time but recovered eventually.'

'So rocking horses are out. Wilf could make a horse on wheels to be pulled along on a rope. Not as exciting but still satisfying.' He grinned. 'I think that the advantage for the child is that an adult has to be there all the time to pull and push and give undivided attention.'

'Last week, I thought of the day-to-day problems and made short-term plans,' Emma said reflectively. 'Now I am beginning to take a longer view and I am halfway there to the States.'

'Don't go too fast. We have a lot to do: banks to visit and visas to get and presentable clothes for the more social occasions.'

'Much of that?'

'On board the *Queen Mary*, and in Washington, and on the lecture tours.'

'The *Queen Mary*?' Emma's eyes widened. 'I've watched her often enough in Cowes

Road and waited for her wash to come over the beach there, several minutes after she passed, but I never dreamed I'd sail in her.'

'She's back to her pre-war state, with all that grey camouflage paint covered with shining black and gleaming funnels again. They say that she looks like a completely different ship. It seems incredible that she was stripped down to be a troop-carrier during the war, and it was a miracle that she escaped German bombs.'

Emma yawned. 'You're right, we have a lot to do. Tomorrow we have invited Robert to coffee while you make plans for the clinic and I start to search the West End for presents. I shall enjoy that.'

Paul switched off the office lights. 'Don't buy the whole of Liberty's, and try to get tickets for Miranda's latest play. Bea is hoping that it will be transferred to America and she can show off her glamorous step-mother.'

'I'll need a lot of spare time. I hope that Eileen can cope with Rose for the day.'

'Tomorrow,' Paul said gently. 'Leave it for now.'

Six

Emma stared at the slim back of the woman disappearing into the theatre. She hurried forward and called, 'Miranda!'

The woman stopped and turned. 'Emma? It's good to see you. What are you doing here?'

'Shopping, and booking for your play. That is if there are seats left for Tuesday night.'

'Wait here. I'll check.'

'Please don't bother. I can ask. I'm sure that you are in a hurry.'

'I want to talk to you, so don't go away.' Miranda smiled and went into the booking office and returned quickly. 'Here. Two dress circle tickets with my compliments.'

'I didn't mean...'

Miranda waved away her thanks. 'Just as well we met. I'm pleased to say we are sold out and my own personal tickets are the only ones left for that evening. Come and have coffee. I have a meeting in half an hour but if I don't have my mid-morning calories, I shall be in trouble with my husband.' She gave a happy laugh. 'He's a tyrant and makes me keep to the diet rigidly. Rehearsals take a lot of energy so I have a small amount of carbohydrate now and balance it with slightly less at lunch-time.'

It was obvious that Miranda was contented in her marriage to Bea's father and from the bloom on her cheeks and the sparkle in her eyes, Emma could see that the diabetic condition was under control.

'You can tell Bea that her wicked step-mother is being very good.' Her expression showed affection for the woman who was so many things to her. 'I owe Bea a great deal. I remember only too well that she nursed me when I was badly in need of stabilising on the newer types of insulin, read the riot act about my future, and put me on the way to self-discipline.' The wide blue eyes were serious. 'She also brought her father to see me again after we'd been apart for too long, and so I live happy ever after, with even more success in my career.'

Emma glanced round the elegantly draped dressing room and smiled. 'You were a success before Bea took you in hand.'

'I am an actress.' Miranda shrugged. 'I was able to show the public a better face than the one I wore backstage. I was sad inside, I was sleeping badly and I felt my stamina slipping away, but now I am fine.'

A girl brought a pot of coffee and a plate of biscuits which Miranda offered to Emma. She took the two biscuits from the other small dish that made up her own allowance and sipped slightly milky coffee.

'Bea enjoyed working with you.'

'She was surprisingly tough and I suspected that if I didn't do as I was told she would ask to be given another private patient to look after.'

'Rubbish. She was doing that for your own good and had no intention of deserting you. Private nursing was a different world and we had to take a lot of initiative in strange surroundings.' Emma looked pensive. 'We didn't do it for long but it was a very interesting time.'

'So I heard,' Miranda said dryly. 'I was talking to one of your patients last month and although he is happily married with three infants and a new hunter of which he is very proud, he had a certain look in his eye when we mentioned you.'

'He must have forgotten me by now.'

'No. He is full of admiration for your help and gentle encouragement when you nursed him, and for pointing out very tactfully that you could never be happy as lady of the manor with horses and dogs ... and his mother. I think you saved his dignity without giving in to what must have been a temptation – wealth and position and the love of a very attractive man.'

'I didn't realise that you knew him well enough to tell you all that! It was rather sad, as I grew really fond of him but knew that I could never marry him. Can you imagine me on the hustings speaking up for him as a future Member of Parliament? His own personality and his war record were enough and his wife is perfect for his way of life.'

'I meet a lot of people in politics now that I'm married to a Member of Parliament myself, and one with a knighthood.' Miranda giggled. 'Makes me doubly famous and the theatre puts a bit of icing on the dull politics, or so I'm told.' She looked at her watch. 'I'm due at rehearsal in five minutes, but I wanted to ask if you are going to see Bea within the forseeable future? She hinted that you are considering it but hadn't done anything about it, to her disgust.'

'Nothing settled but we are working on it.'

'Which could take for ever.' Miranda sighed. 'What I really need is a friend or a nurse companion to come with me to America to see to my diet on the voyage, my injections and my general comfort. When I get over there I shall have my usual dresser, who is flying over a few days later, and she knows all about me and is as strict as my lovely husband, but until then do you know of a nurse who would like a paid working holiday?'

'When are you going and why now?'

'The play is going to America soon. I take the leading role to get it started, then if I tire of it, someone else carries on for six months and I come back here.' For a moment her face clouded. 'I shall have to go alone. When I'm there, I shall be okay but I dread the voyage as I shall have no protection from the press or the public on a liner. I can't stay in my cabin for five days and I could eat the wrong things and have a blip in my health. I'm very good now, but if I am depressed I am not so strict and might eat comfort food.'

'Why not fly?'

'I hate planes and I am air sick.'

'But not seasick?'

'Not that I know of, as yet, and the complete rest for four or five days on board the *Queen Mary* would be a blessing, if I had a companion who would not indulge me in a weakness for cake, and was amusing!'

'I doubt if it would fit in with your arrangements, and I'm not sure when we may go, but Paul is busy choosing a locum to run the practice so that he can fix two lecture tours in the States.'

'Darling! Ring me tonight when you've talked to Paul and if we can't go at the same time, at least give me a name or two if you know any private nurses who are in between jobs.'

A muted bell reminded Miranda that she was due on stage for rehearsal and Emma made her way to the West End shops, but her mind was not on skirts and dresses and blouses. She wandered into the huge offices of the Cunard Line and asked for brochures and timetables of Atlantic crossings on the *Queen Mary*.

'There are other sailings in many of our ships if you need to leave sooner than the *Queen Mary's* next sailing,' Emma was told.

'We did want to go on her, and a friend might want to come with us so there would be three adults and one small child.'

'There is a large suite available on the next voyage, a few first-class single cabins and some doubles, but for your party, the suite might be more suitable and would cost little more than separate first-class cabins.' The clerk was persuasive. 'We can guarantee privacy and extreme comfort. Many famous people use that suite and none of the other ships have anything like it.'

'When would you need to know by?'

'A week before the sailing for confirmation, but we shall be booked up long before she sails in about six weeks. Renovations and redecorations have to be done between sailings and there are still some things to be done now that she is out of wartime camouflage. We try to make a quick turn around, but there are bound to be times when people have to sail in other ships. You do need visas and up-to-date passports for the States,' he pointed out. 'May I pencil in your names, Madam?'

'Just Dr Paul Sykes for now. You can have the other details if we decide to book.' She thought of Miranda and the need to shield her from unwanted publicity on the voyage and wondered if Miranda would have to say what her stage name was as well as being Lady Shuter.

The urge to save money was deeply rooted and Emma found it difficult to spend on luxuries, although wartime limitations were gradually giving way to more plentiful and sometimes frivolous goods in the shops.

The House of Liberty in Regent Street

had always been her favourite store and she recalled with pleasure a time when as an impoverished nurse in training, she had rather diffidently asked about an offer made in the store. If a customer bought dress material, then on coupons and very precious, and bought the pattern for the dress at the same time, an expert would cut out the garment, taking into consideration the exact measurements of the person hoping to wear it, and would add hints as to how it should be sewn. Emma had done this when she saved up to buy some fine pure wool that draped well; the result had been a perfectly fitting black dress that looked as if it came from an exclusive couturier. Dressed up with pearls or bright beads, or sometimes with sprays of felt daisies or swathes of turquoise tulle, it had been her mainstay for social occasions for most of the war.

No such offers today, but Emma bought several lengths of very fine printed cotton that was famous in the store and used for dresses and blouses for people living in, or visiting, hot countries. Bea would have them made up and would revel in the fact that they were unique and very 'English'. She bought silk too, printed with a special design of poppies and cornflowers, a design that she had wanted but never afforded until now.

Muted colours in matt silk and discreet patterns made her smile. These neckties would be perfect for Dwight, who assumed a very British appearance when Bea wanted him to tone down the more brash American clothes that he favoured for casual wear.

After buying shirts for Paul and underwear for herself, the pile of goods became bulky and she treated herself to a taxi back to Kensington.

Mrs Coster greeted her with a hoarse whisper that must have resounded up the stairs to the office. 'He's still here, Sister.'

'Who is?' For a moment, Emma thought that Martin Allen had surfaced again.

'The doctor who is coming here,' Mrs Coster announced with great conviction. 'Took to him the moment he came through that door,' she added dramatically. 'I shall tell my Maureen that he's a real gentleman and I'll have no trouble from him. We'll get on well.'

'That's a relief!' Emma smiled. Mrs Coster sounded as if she had fought off a psychotic rapist and found a knight errant to save her.

A flood of comment threatened and Emma hastily said that she must grab a bite to eat and then go out again. She carried an armful of shopping up to her bedroom and said she'd come for the rest later, then hurried up to the kitchen.

Paul and Robert were sitting on kitchen chairs eating bread and cheese. A good smell of fresh coffee made Emma glance towards the stove. 'We thought you might be back soon,' Paul said. 'Hungry?'

'Starving. I had a full morning and there's more to find but I can go out again as soon as I've had something to eat.'

Robert laughed. 'We haven't eaten all the cheese and I brought this. You need a good ham sandwich.'

'Lovely.' Emma cut bread and made a thick sandwich while Paul poured coffee. 'When can we leave for America?' she asked, and brushed away a few crumbs.

'As soon as you like.'

Emma told them the date of the next sailing of the *Queen Mary* and both men nodded. 'She's in dock having repairs but will be ready in six weeks.' She looked uncertain. 'You did say we'd do it properly and go first-class, but it's expensive.'

'I know.'

'He pencilled in your name but I didn't mention Miranda.'

'Miranda? What has she to do with our going to America? I hope you managed to get tickets for her play?'

'That's when I met her and she insisted on giving us complimentary tickets. The play is being transferred to America and she is going by sea as she hates flying, but dreads being alone. Her husband is tied up in the House and with his job on the War Graves Commission, but her dresser will fly out to meet her.'

'Could she go on that date?'

'Any time within two months. If she is there too early she will visit some friends in New York.'

Paul grinned. 'You really have got the bit between your teeth.' He looked at Robert Forsyth. 'Is that too early for you?'

'Suits me very well. It gives me time to meet a few patients and build up a rapport and give you time to see to your plans.'

'That would help a lot. Move in a few things whenever you like and take it that you are in business! I'd better arrange time off to settle our passage.' Paul smiled. 'What did Miranda really want from you?'

'Not me in particular,' Emma replied defensively. 'She wanted the names of private nurses, one of whom might like a paid passage in return for caring for Miranda's diet and injections.'

'So when you ring her before her matinee, she will know that one very skilled Sister will be there to do everything.'

'She's fun,' Emma retorted. 'It will be a pleasure and she can share the expense of our suite.'

'Suite? And do we dine with the captain?' Paul asked with a hint of irony.

'Oh dear! If Miranda is recognised we might get more attention than we want.'

Robert laughed. 'I'd love to be a fly on the wall. How do you feel about full evening dress every night, Paul?'

'I think I could hate you, Robert! You are a bad influence. You are jealous because you aren't going to escort one of the most beautiful actresses in London.' But Emma was smiling.

'I have other plans closer to home.'

Emma remembered the spark of electricity between Robert and Joan at the dinner party and wondered.

'But that's wonderful, Darling. I shall give an inspired performance today, now that I know you will be with me on the ocean, and a private suite sounds really nice.' Miranda wrote down the date of sailing and said that she was sure that her husband would have time to see them off on the ship.

'So it's another visit to the Cunard office today,' Paul said. 'Only two patients this afternoon and neither of them very serious. Is that all right, throwing you in the deep end, Robert? Mick will see to the notes and be around in the office if you need him. He knows the patients and will be able to tell you as much about them as I can. You'll find him indispensable and very shrewd.'

'It's a good start and I'm very pleased to be available.'

'He's going to set your mind at rest,' Emma said when they got into the car. 'What a relief.'

'Now to business,' Paul told her. 'Visas will be needed and I hope we have time to obtain them.'

'What it is to have important friends. Miranda said she'd ask her husband to get ours when he asks for hers.'

'Good.' Paul handed her a list of things to do. 'Our passports are not out of date and Robert can give us medical certificates to say we have no infection or dire diseases. We need no jabs against typhoid or cholera for where we are going and Rose has had her immunisations done.'

'She enjoyed the anti-polio sugar lump. Quite a surprise treat as she is not allowed sweets between meals.'

'Here we are. I hope they still have that suite available. Have you thought what we call Miranda?'

'I asked her and she wants to be incognito as Lady Shuter.'

'That will save a lot of confusion as that is her name on her passport and if it is on the passenger list, the press might just miss the fact that they have *news* on board.'

'She will have to be interviewed before we reach New York as her agents will insist that she gives publicity to the show opening in America, but a private suite will protect her from casual encounters. Famous people such as Noel Coward sail on that route frequently and they say that the Queen Mother has a great affection for the ship and her crew.'

Paul filled in forms and asked questions and Emma made sure that the booking clerk made a note that Lady Shuter was a diabetic and that she would give a diet sheet to the catering department to be followed rigidly. 'We shall also need sterilising facilities for the needles and glass and metal syringes used for insulin injections as Lady Shuter will not bring an unlimited supply of sterile material with her.'

Nothing seemed a problem and they emerged from the office with a sensation of achievement mixed with a slightly guilty feeling that they were going to move in very expensive and elevated circles.

'I shall grow lazy, surrounded by luxury, and I may even be able to wear that gold watch and chain from my grandfather. Up to now I haven't had the paunch to show it off, but I intend to eat everything that's fattening and expand into a dignified figure.'

Emma gave him a dirty look. 'I believe that Dwight had all the latest gymnasium equipment installed to make sure that he stays slim.'

'Good, we don't want you to lose your lovely figure.'

An air of light-hearted independence made them laugh as they made their way back to the car. Nobody would recognise them as an eminent psychiatrist and a skilled nursing sister with a family and responsibilities. They looked young and very happy.

'It's so exciting,' breathed Emma. 'Until

we really signed and booked our passage, I only half believed it would ever come true, but now I shall plan, make endless lists and I can't wait to tell Bea the news.'

'Most of the shopping and arrangements will have to be your duty,' Paul reminded her. 'I have lectures to assemble and contacts to make in the States. I know the outline of my itinerary but it needs firming up and suddenly there is no time at all to do everything.'

'You have masses of material. Your collection of case histories alone, and the results, are proof of your status.'

'They need reviewing and making sure that real names and locations are not used. Some of the earlier cases who have responded well want to forget that they ever had the stigma of mental illness, however much we reassure them that they were ill and not mad.'

'The functional disorders which were just a resistance to the trauma of life? like Dwight's conviction that he had dropped the bomb on Hiroshima and therefore should not have children? I think that the medics in the States will learn a lot from your wartime cases of battle fatigue.'

Emma did more shopping and Paul bought several latest editions of textbooks that he wanted to show to his contacts in America, and they arrived home as Robert was putting down the phone and pushing his notes together.

'It went well,' he announced with satisfaction. 'Mick is helpful and isn't afraid to give his private opinion to back up my diagnosis.' He grinned. 'Very pungent, some of his remarks, but relevant.'

'Any calls?'

'Two new appointments made through local doctors and one call from a woman who wanted to speak to you personally. She refused to give a name and sounded cross that you were not here, but when I asked if she was a patient, she sounded as if I'd suggested something obscene!'

Paul shook his head. 'Could be anyone. If it's urgent she'll ring again.'

'You'll stay and eat with us?' Emma suggested. 'You are a part of the establishment now.'

'Not tonight. I must clear up in my flat and bring more things over. See you tomorrow.' He gathered his papers and briefcase and they heard his car start. 'I must baby-sit for Eileen,' Emma decided. 'It is her night for the cinema and I think Mick wants to see the film too. We can have omelettes and salad and fresh fruit after I've put the babes to bed.'

'We'll wait until it's reasonable to ring Bea. I think the last time we called, we woke her up. The time zones take a bit of getting used to.'

'She was glad to hear from us. One of the twins had a bad cold and she was sitting with him and was very bored.'

Paul glanced at the notes that Robert had made and was satisfied. Everything would be safe in his hands and even Mick had been impressed.

He selected twenty case histories that he would need to monitor if the patients were to remain incognito and began the work to retype them under new names. Mick would do some of the work if he had the pencilled alterations to follow and with luck the work could be done quickly.

The phone rang and broke his chain of thought. 'Dr Sykes.'

A female voice sounded cautious. 'You really are Dr Sykes?'

'Of course.'

'What I have to ask is confidential.'

'May I have your name and do you wish to make an appointment to see me?'

'I'm not coming to you as a patient. All I want is information about a friend.'

'Unless I know who you are and what your authority is to ask details of what is a private matter between doctor and patient, I can't help. I'd rather not be told the name of the patient but is this person a patient in this clinic?'

'So I hear.' The voice was spiteful. 'And not only your patient if what I hear is true.'

'You really must not ask about anyone who comes here,' Paul pointed out again. 'Why not ask the person concerned?'

'She refuses to tell me, but I know that she has been to see you and she was seen coming away from the Princess Beatrice Hospital one morning.'

'Hundreds of people go there for a variety of reasons,' he said gently.

'Not through that entrance.'

'What entrance?'

'The one that leads to the block where they treat prostitutes.' The venom was even more pronounced. 'The one by the side gates.'

'The one marked Medical Unit?'

'Yes,' she said eagerly.

'Have you read the whole notice there? It also leads to the X-ray Department, Skin Unit and Physiotherapy, if I remember rightly.'

'They treat venereal diseases there and I know that she is a dirty little whore.'

'That is a serious accusation.'

'It's true. My brother went about with her and now he's got syphilis.'

Paul felt cold and in a quandary, torn between his vow of patient confidentiality and his public duty to expose the source of infection. 'I can tell you nothing about any patient who attends my clinics. I have no idea why you ask me, as I do not treat venereal diseases. Anyone attending the clinic you mention is protected against casual enquiries, but they are treated, and contacts are found and warned or treated if infected. Your brother must tell his own doctor if he is sure of the source of his infection but there is no way that a third party can obtain such information from me or anyone else involved.' He hesitated. 'It would have to be established that she was the only one who could have given him the condition. Do you have proof that she does have the disease? A man who takes a lot of partners must be careful who he accuses, as must you.'

'There have been other women but I just know it's her and not one of them. Thinks herself somebody special and he is nuts about her, but once I've found out the truth he'll never want to see her again.'

'You must speak to your brother and he must tell his own doctor, but I cannot help you.'

'I'll see her damned! You doctors are all alike, you gang up with each other and tell what lies you want but I'll get even with her.'

'You'd better tell me her name,' he asked reluctantly.

'Not likely, now that I can see you all stick together.' She slammed down the phone and Paul sat heavily in his leather chair, more uneasy than he'd been for months over a patient. He was sure he knew who the patient was and he had heard from 'A' Block at Beatties that she had admitted a string of names who might be infected. That was under control. What scared him was the anger and venom that came over the telephone line and the feeling that violence could be in the air.

Seven

'What's up, Doc?'

'Did you take a call from a woman yesterday who refused to give her name?'

'Yes. I handed it over to Dr Forsyth, who told her you were away. She wouldn't leave a message as she said you were the one who knew about the case. A bit fishy I thought. Like that man who wanted to know what was wrong with one of his employees so he'd have an excuse to sack him.'

'This was worse. Be extra careful if she rings again. She was very angry and might cause a lot of trouble. I must put Forsyth in the picture when he comes in. I have a shrewd suspicion that she is trying to find out about the lady I referred to 'A' block.'

Mick whistled. 'No need to worry about her, Doc. She'll make her own bed of nettles if she can't control herself, but when she comes here again you can only repeat your warning to be careful, if that's possible for her. That's all anyone can do.'

'She's much better now that she is lightly sedated and she knows about her uncle and her childhood and I think she's beginning to control her passions. In a way she is fastidious, and the thought of disease horrified her.'

'Like everybody, it couldn't happen to her!'

'She is responding to treatment in 'A' block and will come here for only a few more sessions of analysis. Forsyth can cope with them. She was very upset when I told her what came out of the hypnosis and genuinely wants to put the past behind her.'

'I bet she's scared. Maybe that's her cure. Like in the Army, nobody thought they'd get a dose and it couldn't happen to them, and when it did there was hell to pay when they went home and had to tell the wife.' Mick grinned. 'Some poor bastards thought that having an FFI examination when they came back from a night out waved a magic wand and was a treatment in itself, so they couldn't get anything really bad wrong with them for sleeping with a dirty woman.'

'The Free From Infection inspection is still valuable, if only to diagnose the conditions that can now be treated with penicillin.'

'A real miracle drug, Doc, but I'm glad I never chased skirt. I wouldn't have Eileen and Jean if I had.'

'We have work to do.' Paul handed Mick a sheaf of papers. 'Use your imagination and type these again using fancy names and placing them firmly in Dundee or Belfast, Timbuktu or any place far from here.'

'I'll ask Eileen for names. She has a fancy for double-barrelled names and I'll have to watch out that she doesn't suggest the names of her favourite film stars. We don't want Ronald Colman accused of being a psychopath,' he added cheerfully.

Paul went to see his first patient and was joined by Robert an hour later while Emma looked through the clothes that she hoped would still be big enough for Rose when they went to America. The boxes of bright new sandals were ready to be packed and would fill a small case, as Bea had sent the outlines of her children's feet so that Emma could buy some for them too.

Emma laughed. 'Red sandals seem to be the fashion for the very young. Rose said that the other colours hurt and Bea asked for red, too.'

'I bought some pretty pink shoes in the market,' Eileen said, 'but they rub Jean's heels and Mick was ever so cross when I told him, so I had to buy some like you did, and the lady in the shop measured Jean's feet and put them under some kind of X-ray machine. They look too big to me, but she said they were her right size and I suppose she thinks she knows, but the pink ones are so pretty.'

'Mick is in the office by the phone and the doctors are busy and don't need us, so let's take both the girls into the park and they can wear their new sandals.'

Emma could ill afford the time, as she had many things to do, but she wanted to make sure that Eileen allowed Jean to wear the right shoes. Eileen was only too eager to make her child look pretty, and sacrificed comfort and practicality for her idea of glamour. Shades of Shirley Temple and the other early child stars, Emma thought. How many unfortunate babies had suffered their bouncy hair to be tortured into stiff ringlets and made to wear short white socks meant for sunny California, even when the weather was cold in an English spring breeze?

Dressed in a warm coat of cream wool, edged with a pale blue velvet collar and trimmings, tailored in a version of a double-breasted adult topcoat, Rose looked smart and very sweet. Her gloves hung from a cord threaded through the sleeves and behind the neck so that she couldn't lose them and the red sandals were almost over bright over the warm, cream stockings.

Eileen looked at her own daughter with reservation. 'The sun is warm, isn't it? I did want her to look nice and wear that woolly I knitted but the last time she went out without a coat, she cried and said she was cold.'

'That child will have another cold if you don't watch out,' Mrs Coster said accusingly. 'Run and get a coat for the poor mite while I get out the pushchairs.'

Emma gave her a pleased glance as Mrs Coster had voiced her own thoughts but she tried not to find fault with anything that Eileen did for her own child.

The red sandals were a great success once the little girls had overcome their distrust of the first stiffness of the soles and Eileen forgot that Jean was muffled up in a brown jacket and couldn't show the orange jumper, lovingly knitted but quite hideous.

Luigi, as usual, gave each child a biscuit when they passed the restaurant and as usual asked the mothers when they would be producing more children. 'They both need brothers to keep them in order,' he said, and lightly boxed his son's ear for stealing a biscuit.

'He is awful,' Eileen giggled as they pushed the now silent, biscuit-chewing children home. 'The nerve, talking about such things. It's none of his business, but Mick would still like a little boy so that he can play at trains and aeroplanes.'

'What do you think of it?'

'I'm not keen. I love my Jean and if I have another I hope it will be another girl, but I don't want to be fat and ugly again for months and months, so I keep putting it off.'

Emma ignored the glance that said that she was doing the same as Eileen. 'You looked very pretty when you were carrying Jean.'

Eileen blushed. 'Mick seemed to think so. He kept saying that I looked like that Italian film star with the big bust and he was quite disappointed when it all went after I finished feeding the baby.'

'Men like curves and you still have a good figure.'

'That's as maybe but I told him he'd have to wait for a son until you and Dr Paul come back from America.'

Emma smiled. Eileen had made every excuse possible to avoid having another baby and this was the best line she had managed for months, but was she any worse than Emma? There was no real reason why she should wait if she wanted more children. A chance meeting with Stella, the obstetrician who had delivered Rose had made Emma realise that too great a gap before she was pregnant again mightn't be good for Rose.

What had Stella hinted? That an only child could easily be spoiled and be too demanding. Looking at Rose's smiling and contented face, Emma dismissed the idea, but she noticed that the two little girls now played far more self-centred games and had begun to share less of their toys.

'Help me go over Rose's clothes,' Emma suggested. 'If we are away for a long time, she will grow out of a lot of what fits well now, and the climate over there is different so you must take what will be too small for her shortly and let Jean get the benefit from them.'

'Do you want to keep that nice dress?' asked Eileen. 'You never let her wear it and it's ever so pretty.'

Emma bit back the remark that it was not right for Rose and unfolded it. A patient who said she was a dress designer and loved making children's clothes had brought it and insisted on seeing Rose in it. The harsh yellows of the fabric decorated with green leaf sprays had robbed the child of all her vibrant colour and the lace dripping from the collar and cuffs was limp and reminded Emma of pictures of consumptive Victorian women.

'You really like it?' she asked, unable to hide her disbelief. Hastily, she added, 'It's too big just now but if you want it, take it and keep it for Jean.'

'It's brand new!'

'So is this but Rose doesn't like it.' Is Rose being allowed to have her own way too much? she wondered.

Eileen went off happily hugging a bundle of clothes and Emma packed up the pretty, smocked Vyella dresses and smooth pastel knitted cardigans that would suit any climate.

The long evening dresses that Emma had worn a few times seemed to belong to a make-do-and-mend era. The inventiveness that most women had shown when clothes were rationed and supplies of cloth were scarce was now unnecessary. She looked at a picture in *Vogue* magazine and caught her breath. The crimson silk dress with masses of material in the skirt and the high ruched bodice and tight waistline that accentuated the model's bosom would be perfect for use on the *Queen Mary,* and for Washington if what Bea had told her was true.

'Buy it,' Paul said when she showed him the picture. 'It says there which shops have that model, or there must be many similar styles that would suit you.' He grinned. 'How am I to live up to having two glamorous women with me?'

'I need a tailored suit more,' Emma said reluctantly.

'We have money, and you have money of your own which you never spend on yourself. Why not see Miranda after the play and ask if she can go with you on a day when she has no matinee?'

'I'll be delighted,' Miranda told her, in her dressing room. 'I need some cocktail dresses, and a suit if the weather is cold there. I shall have to travel to promote the play and I've been told that I may have to be filmed for television. Can't say I want that. A friend who was interviewed said that they made her up with terribly thick cream and she felt as if her skin would crack when she smiled. She had to wear green eyeshadow that made her look, as she said, as if she had two newt's armpits above her eyes. The very bright lights make complexions look like dingy leather unless they pile on the make-up and the American actresses favour much heavier mascara and very bright red lipstick. My husband says that he could never kiss a woman with all that mess on her face, so maybe I shall make him come to America where he'll be safe from temptation.'

She turned from her mirror, the last vestiges of the cold cream that removed her stage make-up glowing on her smooth skin. She wiped it off with a soft cloth and applied a light vanishing cream and a dusting of powder.

'We won't keep you,' Paul said. 'The play will be a great success everywhere you take it but it wouldn't be the same without you. You were superb.'

'Thank you, Darling.' Miranda kissed Paul and hugged Emma. 'See you on Friday,' she said.

'Shopping with Miranda is like being taken along in a whirlwind,' Emma said as she sank into a chair surrounded by her packages. We went to five major stores and a boutique.'

'She looks so fragile,' Paul said with a grin.

'It helps to know what you want and not to be intimidated by snooty saleswomen. She sat on a gilt chair and demanded what she wanted without stirring a finger and let everyone else do the panicking. Surrounded by lovely clothes I was confused and I had to feel fabrics, wonder if the garment would fit me and try them all on before deciding, but she had a list of measurements and colour preferences and made it clear that she was not going to waste time trying on anything that she didn't choose. Finally, she gathered what she wanted and fitted on a few while I tried not to be persuaded to buy a dress I hated but which the saleswoman said would be *divine* with my colouring.'

'You seem to have bought a few things all the same.' Paul eyed the pile of bags with mock alarm. 'Are we going to afford America after this?'

Emma laughed. 'Bea once told me that Miranda would be wonderful haggling with Arab traders. She bought three dresses and I bought a long evening gown and a short cocktail dress, then Miranda calmly asked what discount they would give us as if she expected one as a matter of course. 'Don't pack the dresses until I know what I am paying,' she said sweetly to the girl. 'Ask your superior and tell her that at least one of the dresses will appear when I take the play to the States, that is if I decide to buy.' She then looked at her wrist watch and declared, 'We have other places to visit. I think that Harvey Nichols will be good for suits."

'What happened?'

'It was so funny. A very stiff and smartly dressed woman came and tried to look very formidable but Miranda smiled and looked at her watch again, saying that she really didn't have all day to waste on a few clothes. Almost meekly, a generous discount was offered, and Miranda said she'd call back for the clothes when they were parcelled up.'

'So, what are you going to do next? I can see that you are restless and if you pack and unpack too many times you will have to press all the clothes again!'

'It's all very well for you, as you have to tell Robert so much and tie up the loose ends with the others who will help with your private patients, but Mrs Coster's Maureen helps Eileen now, leaving me a lot of time for Rose and myself.'

'When you thought you'd be busy preparing for the voyage you decided you'd be overworked,' Paul agreed, 'but we should have realised that your normal efficiency would mop up any extra work quickly and here you are, twiddling your thumbs!'

'What do you suggest? I'm too restless to start sewing again and we've given dinner parties to everyone we like, saying we are going away.'

'Go down to Emily. Don't say that there isn't time for that. You have a couple of spare weeks and could go for a long weekend or even a whole week. Take Rose and relax.'

'Aunt Emily would be thrilled, and Rose adores her.'

'Wilf can leave your old car at the end of

the pier for you and you have a spare key.'

'The car might be a bit reluctant to start after all this time.'

'Actually...' Paul began.

'You've already spoken to Aunt Emily!'

'I did talk to her last night. She said that she lent your car to George when he came to her a few weeks ago with Clive. He changed the oil and saw to the electrics and it is as good as new, or almost.'

'So when is she expecting me,' Emma asked dryly.

'Tomorrow? Ring tonight and tell her you'll be on the late morning ferry. Rose will like going by train. I wish I could come too.'

'It's a very good idea. Eileen has to get used to me being away and she can be really in charge of Mrs Coster and Maureen and everything for a while, but still be able to ask me anything that puzzles her when I come back and before we go away for a long time.'

'Daddy come too?' Rose asked for the third time the following day.

'Not this time, precious. You are going on the train and Aunt Emily will be on the island to see you and let you play with Noah's Ark.'

'All the animals?'

'All of them if you are careful. Poor Wilf had to make another sheep as you lost one the last time you played with them.'

'He ran away,' Rose protested.

'Perhaps you'll find him this time, Little Bo Peep!'

Mick drove them to Paddington Station, bought a platform ticket from a penny-in-the-slot machine and settled them in the train with their luggage, which was decidedly less than when Emma had nappies and cot blankets to take with them. By the time they reached Portsmouth Harbour, Rose had looked at three books, drawn an animal that she said was a horse and drunk a small bottle of orange juice.

Emma put reins on the excited child when the train stopped, opened the pushchair and loaded the case onto it, and they walked to the ferry terminal. Rose almost fell over, trying to look up at the wheeling seagulls and when they were on the ferry demanded to be released from the reins, but Emma firmly kept her well under control and after a few minutes Rose found so much to see that she forgot that she was tethered.

The last of the rusting iron sea defences had gone and the buildings on the seafront at Ryde were sparkling with new paint to spruce up the town, ready for summer visitors who now trickled back as the dinginess of the war years was put behind them. As Emma drove to the house near Shide where Aunt Emily lived, she passed several houses with bed and breakfast signs in the windows. She sighed with pleasure, remembering the hordes of holiday-makers who came to the island before the war. Everything was recovering and the future looked bright.

Wilf, Emily's handyman waved to Emma to stop at the corner of the path that led to her own cottage. 'Thought you'd be on that ferry,' he said, as if he had seen her very recently and her arrival was no surprise. 'Miss Darwen has a full house so you'll be staying in your own place this time. I've lit a couple of fires and the beds are made and there's milk and bread in the larder with some eggs and things for breakfast. Miss Darwen wants you to go up to the house for midday dinner and she'll tell you all about it.'

'Who is staying there?' Emma called, but Wilf waved her through the gateway and walked away behind the coal bunker.

'I expect that Aunt Janey is with Aunt Emily,' she said to Rose. 'I wonder if she's brought Clive with her?'

'Clive!' Rose darted away in the direction of Emily Darwen's house and would not come back when Emma called. Emma shrugged and returned to her unpacking. Rose would come to no harm and she was very fond of her big cousin. Bad luck to Rose if Aunt Emily had other guests. She couldn't take it for granted that they were the only people to descend on her at a day's notice.

Emma banked up the fire in the small sitting-room so that it could be stirred into flame when they returned from the house. The smell of burning applewood was a memory of other visits to the island and her expression was soft when she strolled up the lane leading to the home of her favourite aunt.

'Mummy!' Rose ran to meet her and hung on to her hand. 'Come and see Clive. I want a spade.'

Clive was digging potatoes from the clamp at the end of the garden and from the state of Rose's shoes, it was evident that she'd been helping him.

'Have you said hello to Aunt Emily?'

'No.' Rose stood uncertainly by the pile of potatoes, torn between her desire to see her great-aunt and to stay with Clive, who was surprisingly tolerant for a young boy and was really fond of his little cousin.

'Go on,' Clive said. 'I've finished now and I want to come in for some milk.'

Rose ran to the house calling for her Aunt Emmy in a loud voice, and Emma followed her into the kitchen.

A masculine voice said, 'You can't go in there yet. Take off those filthy sandals and let me clean them. Now you can go,' he added and Emma saw her daughter dance away in stockinged feet while George held her muddy sandals. He grinned. 'I think I recognise you but it's been so long since we met that I'd almost forgotten how pretty you are ... almost.'

'I didn't expect to see you here,' Emma said. 'When do you get married?'

'Soon.' His smile was softer now. 'It's about time, or so they tell me. You will like her, Emma. She has a certain smile that dimples one cheek, just as your smile does.'

'Let me take those shoes,' Emma said, forbidding the treacherous dimple to appear.

'I'll do these. You are in charge of cabbages. Aunt Emily needs two as they are small and I'll help Clive bring in the potatoes.'

'Where is she?'

'In there with my mother, talking as usual. You'd think they never saw each other from one year's end to the next.' He bent forward and whispered. 'Go and see her or they'll think I've abducted you.'

'Idiot,' she said, her dimple showing, and left him staring after her.

Eight

Emma prodded the potatoes and said that they were done and Emily basted the joint of pork for the last time. 'Did Dr Sutton have another grateful farmer patient?' Emma asked.

'I'm glad you are all here. I'd never have finished it on my own and Wilf doesn't like pork.' Emily laughed. 'I know who will have some cold. Dr Sutton gives me too much on purpose as he likes coming to supper to have cold pork and home-made chutney.'

'You should have married him years ago,' Janey said. 'I suppose you made extra stuffing for him too. Does he eat all that?'

George looked at his mother with a wicked smile. 'Why not make Mother happy and we can have a double wedding. She hasn't had a good cry at a wedding for ages.'

'That will be quite enough of that kind of talk,' Emily said sternly. 'You can all go back over the water if you go on like that. Emma and I can have a bit of peace.'

'Not with Rose around,' Emma said. 'Where have they gone?'

'Turning out the play box,' George said. 'Clive found a very dirty wooden sheep in the potato clamp and they are putting it back with the other animals, washed and a bit blackened but otherwise none the worse. Leave them while we eat and they can have something when they are hungry. They may need drying off as Wilf gave Clive a model boat that they found fascinating. They sailed it in the bath with a lot of splashing to make-believe rough seas.'

The tension that Emma had expected when she met George again wasn't there and he seemed very much at ease with the cousin he had been in love with for so long. They talked of his coming wedding and he showed no sign that he was relieved or disappointed when Emma told him that she would not be there but would be in America.

'I must try to think of a suitable wedding present,' Emma said. 'Perhaps I'll leave it until I am in America unless you can tell me what Margaret would like?'

'We like surprises,' he said and grinned. 'I must give Paul a few addresses of naval friends. America is a big place and a few widely scattered contacts can be useful,' he offered. 'Margaret will have to meet you later, when we come to London.'

'Robert Forsyth will make you welcome if we aren't there. He is moving in this week and it's as if he's been working with us for a long time instead of a few days. It's such a relief for Paul as the other applicants for the job were not suitable at all and we were afraid we'd lose Mick and Eileen if the right person wasn't found. It was a shattering experience to find that one applicant isn't even a qualified doctor but was so pushy he hoped he had convinced us that he could do the work. Why not arrange with Robert for you to stay at the house for a while when you come back from your honeymoon? There's masses of room.'

'We'll bear that in mind but I have to get back to work and so does Margaret. She will stay in the Navy for a while and Mother is going to carry on looking after Clive.'

'Clive is no trouble at all,' Janey said, with an air of defiance, as if someone had doubted her abilities to cope with a lively small boy with an enquiring mind and loads of energy. 'I love him dearly and dread the day when you will take him away.'

Emily brought in a steamed pudding with golden syrup and Janey served it, but her hand was weak and she spilled some hot syrup on the tablecloth. Quietly, George took the serving spoon and finished filling the dishes and Emily looked worried.

'Emma and I can wash up,' she said firmly. 'I want to talk to her as it's been months since she was here.'

'We'll go for a walk as far as the station,' George said. 'Is that too far for you, Mother? I can handle the children and they both love the trains.'

'Nothing wrong with my legs,' Janey retorted, 'just my hands.'

'Her arthritis is very bad,' Emma said, as soon as she was splashing hot water into the sink and swishing the cotton head of the washing-up mop through the water. The mesh container filled with scraps of soap that Emily used to soften the water for washing up was a remnant of wartime frugality and Emma was amused to see the bar of soap for hand washing had a backing of silver paper to keep one side of the bar from dissolving when in use.

'Janey's hands are getting worse. I had a touch of rheumatism but nothing really bad, but Janey has a lot of pain and can't hold heavy dishes. She's afraid of having an accident but she's too proud to ask for help.'

'Is she able to look after Clive? She sounded as if someone had told her that she can't do that for much longer.'

'That was her nosy neighbour who is liable to rub anyone up the wrong way, but Alex told her to mind her own business, which is a surprise as he is such a mild man. He is very good to Janey and helps her a lot. Alex retired and sold the marine instrument firm so that he can be with her and take his part in looking after Clive, and they have a nanny and help with the cleaning, so she can manage and I never hint otherwise. Clive is a big boy now and does a lot for himself.'

Emily Darwen laughed. 'As one door closes, another opens, or so I've always believed. George is lucky to have Margaret. Next year when she has her first baby, she will leave the service and take over making a home for George, Clive and the baby brother.'

'A baby boy? So soon?'

'Yes. They will want a child quickly to make their lives complete and it will be a boy. Margaret is a very wise woman. She knows that George has a dread of losing her as he lost Sadie, and she knows about you,' she added with a wry smile. 'Both of them have loved and lost or not been able to have their heart's desire and even if Sadie died of meningitis and not in childbirth, the dread is still there for him. He has lost too much in life. If she is to have a husband who looks at her and no other woman and feels secure in their marriage, she must make it happen.' Her eyes were dark, as if she saw visions. 'She will care for Janey too, which is a blessing. They really like each other and Margaret looks on Janey as her own mother, as her family died in the Blitz and her only relative is an ancient aunt by marriage who lives in Scotland.

'What about Alex? Does he miss the business?' Emma asked quietly, sensing that once again Emily knew the future.

'Alex will be busy turning one very big house into two apartments. He is good at that and renovation of property has always a been a hobby when he had leave from the Navy. He spoke to me about it last month and has a house in mind. I saw it coming. Either they will live in one half and let the other, with a lot of help in the house for Janey, or Margaret and the children will live in the other half ready for George when he is home on leave and yet have a care for Janey. They will have a willing child-minder if they want to go away.'

Emma watched the thin hands wiping the dishes. There were more liver spots than she recalled but the fingers were flexible and strong. 'You don't have arthritis,' she remarked.

'I get the screws in my knees at times but nothing much.' Emily shrugged. 'I've never been able to sit still for long enough for my joints to stiffen.'

'It's the hard stuff that keeps you going.' Emma said, giggling.

'You may laugh, but I know it does me good and it helps Janey's hands to hurt less when she has some in her tea. She hates taking medicine for her rheumatics and I've been making an ointment that my mother used to make for a friend with bad rheumatism.'

'Is that it?' Emma bent over the iron pot on the stove. A thick, almost solid concoction was warm and fragrant with herbs. 'Smells good enough to eat.'

'I need some more bark and leaves. There's a copse by the mill and we could walk down and get some. Put on gumboots as the sides of the stream are marshy. You can help me pick some but we'll leave the children with George and Janey when they come back from their walk as it's far too muddy where we are going and they've got wet enough for one day, playing with that wretched boat. I'll have words with Wilf over that! We'll slip out the back way without the children seeing us.'

Emma knew that her aunt wanted to be

alone with her as she would miss her when she was in the States, so she pulled on the pair of wellingtons that almost fitted, and followed Emily out into the back garden, through the bushes to the lane and down to the mill.

'It's never used now is it?' Emma asked, gazing up at the tapering ivy-covered walls and the remnants of the upper storey where once grain had been stored and the miller and his family had lived.

'The force of the water grew less with the years as the stream silted up and the last miller died in my mother's time. We came here as children to play in the stream and to pick watercress if the gypsies left any. They hawked the bunches in Newport and sold a lot to our shop. I heard that the floor was rotten and that it all had to be boarded up to prevent anyone from falling through, but tramps do get in and use it for shelter sometimes. They'll set it on fire one day if they try to keep warm and use the dry floorboards for fuel. Otherwise they do no harm and the police take no notice.'

'What are we trying to find?'

'Willows by the water. I want leaves and bark to grind and slim stems which I can peel and steep the scrapings until they are soft, then I boil it all up and add it to the lanolin base.'

'Is that all?' Emma said dryly. 'It sounds like hard work. Can't you buy an ointment?'

'There are unguents but this will do better. I add rosemary and lavender to make it smell sweet which in itself is soothing and a few leaves of bay and some other things that Mother said were good.' She giggled. 'My trade secret, and when it's put through a strainer and is smooth and set, nobody can tell what goes into it. Dr Sutton says I ought to patent it. I don't think he admits where he gets it, but it has done a lot of good to two of his patients.'

'Willow?' Emma thought for a moment. 'Of course. Salix! Salicylic acid ... aspirin for rheumatism.'

'Probably. Nothing to get excited about,' Emily said composedly. 'Whatever it is does some good.'

Emma stripped long, pointed leaves from a tree and picked twigs but left the remains of the willow catkins as Emily didn't need them. They gathered bay leaves from the bush in the garden and she wondered who had discovered the healing properties of herbs years ago.

'You must look at my Culpeper. That book has a lot of sense and I've used it several times over the years and especially during the two wars. Men came home with wounds that didn't heal properly even after they'd been in hospital and yet the men were better in every other way. I helped a good few old wounds, just with honey, and others with seaweed,' she said quietly. 'Doctors don't know everything as I tell Dr Sutton sometimes when he gets on his high horse about some folk remedy or other.'

'Does he know you are a witch?'

'Stop teasing me and put the kettle on. I need a cup of tea after all that walking.'

'Where did you go?' Janey asked.

'I needed some herbs and Emma doesn't mind standing in mud if she has gumboots. I'm afraid I'll slip so I try to get someone else to pick my leaves.'

Janey stirred the iron pot. 'Is it ready?'

Emily tossed in the torn bay leaves. 'Not quite. Here's a job for you, George. Mash the willow leaves and scrape the twigs and add all that to the pot, and leave it to simmer while we have tea. It will be ready to take away tomorrow morning when you go home, Janey.'

The children played happily with Noah's Ark and a book about cats and after tea Rose was sleepy enough to want to go to bed. Emma put her in the pushchair and said good-night.

'We have to go back in the morning,' Janey said. 'Alex will need me and George has to go back on duty.'

'Come to breakfast,' Emily suggested. 'You can drive them to the ferry. What about supper? If Rose is in bed, you can't come up here and leave her but I can send something down.'

'I don't need anything,' Emma assured her. 'I have those lovely fresh eggs and bread and cheese that you left in the cottage and I'm a bit tired too.'

'You can move in here when the others are gone,' Emily suggested. 'If Rose goes to bed early and you are in the cottage, I'll see nothing of you unless I come down there and I like my own fireside.'

The cottage was warm and the fire needed only a touch with the brass poker to ease it into flame. The smaller grate in the little bedroom that Rose used gave out enough heat to take the chill off the air and Rose was almost asleep when Emma undressed her and tucked her up in bed with her favourite knitted cat.

Outside the back door, a hen, escaped from the neighbouring farm, made self-satisfied crowings and pecked at the cabbage leaves that Wilf had left on the compost heap. Emma smiled. Even the hen would be safe here and find its way home when it was tired of rummaging, unless a fox was about at night.

London faded from her mind as she slept and the absence of traffic made the night soft.

The friendly sounds of the country woke her early and she listened to the awakened world of small animals. It would be wonderful to live here, she decided, then heard Rose talking to herself in the next room. When small arms hugged her and a moist kiss on her cheek said good morning, she knew it could never be true until Rose grew up and Paul gave up his work in Kensington, but so long as they were together, it would never be a problem where they lived.

'Anyone awake?'

Emma looked out of the bedroom window and waved. George sat on the broken bench by the kitchen window and Clive trailed a stick along the railings by the path, making a very satisfactory metallic drumming noise. 'We'll be ready in five minutes,' Emma called.

'Clive! Clive,' called Rose and impatiently tried to help Emma dress her but made no fuss as her arms were thrust into garment sleeves and her shoes were buckled firmly.

'Now you can go,' Emma said and Rose ran out into the garden to see Clive.

The hen had decided that Emma's garden was more peaceful than the farm and sat on a pile of dry leaves by the flower-bed.

George put a careful hand under her and laughed. 'For my next trick! Ta-ra!' He brought out an egg and handed it to Emma. 'I think she's getting broody so we'll take her back to the farm in case she is lost. Put Rose in her pushchair and we can go while you help the others with breakfast.'

With amusement, Emma watched the strange little procession: Clive pushing Rose in her stroller and George with an unprotesting hen under his arm and an egg in his hand walking slowly with the two children. A wave of affection made her want to be with them but she held back and went to the house knowing that George was being wise. He kept contact with her to a minimum even now that he had Margaret to love and to marry soon.

Emily gave Emma a sharp glance. 'Where are they?'

'Taking a hen back to the farm,' Emma replied. 'No need to look at me like that. I have done nothing to inflame old passions. He thinks that a broody hen is far more exciting than Emma Sykes.'

'I'm glad you came,' Emily said. 'He

needed to see you just once more in familiar surroundings before he marries Margaret and both Janey and I think he's almost over you. Not entirely,' she warned, 'but enough to set him free.'

'Paul likes him and I am very fond of him. I feel a real sense of family now and I think he is beginning to feel the same, as a cousin, so we hope to see something of them after the wedding.'

'I've looked out the lace for Bea and her mother-in-law. In her last letter she said that the Americans go mad over handmade lace.'

'And you took the hint!'

'Bea is all right,' Emily said, as if she needed to justify the deep affection she had for the ebullient and beautiful woman. 'I'd love to see you meet again, and you can give my love to Dwight. He's all right, too.'

'Praise indeed,' Emma replied dryly.

'What are you taking over there?'

'Dress material from Liberty's and sandals for the twins and Mark. I wish I could take more but those are the things I know she needs and can't get over there. Miranda bullied me into buying some rather nice clothes for myself and it will be fun having her with us on the voyage.'

'Have you decided on which boat you sail?'

'The *Queen Mary*. It's all arranged and you can wave if she goes out on this side of the Solent.'

'I'm glad. Somehow she is a part of the life here. I saw her when she started on her maiden voyage in the thirties. Hundreds of small craft sailed round her and followed her as far as the Needles, and the men in the docks went nearly mad with pride. She looked really grand and somehow even during the war when she was used as a troop-ship in dangerous waters, I knew she'd come to no real lasting harm.'

'She's back to her normal colours now they say. The grey camouflage paint was useful on the grey Atlantic but I want to see her gleaming with red and white and black paint again. I must see if I still have the brooch you gave me that you bought in Cowes on that occasion. Maybe I should wear it or pin it to Rose's coat.'

'I'd forgotten. Your mother bought one too

but of course hers had to be bigger and brighter,' Emily said with a sniff.

'I wore it pinned to my beret and tried to look like Jean Harlow.' Emma giggled. 'I wonder what film stars Rose will find as fascinating in a year or so.'

'So long as she doesn't fall in love with one of those boys who wear clothes copied from the Edwardians. What started as an elegant fashion is becoming common, with the wrong sort wearing it now.'

'You are a snob, Aunt Emily. I met some of the Teddy boys in London when I went to Beatties to see Joan Bright and most of them are only showing off. Everyone has to have someone to admire and they try to be different. Some of the clothes are really expensive and when they keep them clean and well brushed they are really smart.'

Emily looked disbelieving. 'I heard that they have gangs who fight and do a lot of damage.'

'That happens in every generation and now that most of the young men have been demobbed they are bored. Cheer up! By the time that Rose gets interested in boys, something else will be the fashion and we may find that the next lot are very staid and good.'

'You are too optimistic. Be careful when you are in America. I hear it is a very wicked place, with people being robbed in broad daylight.'

'Confess. You don't see anything bad for me, do you?' Emma asked gently.

'No, that's true, but it doesn't mean you can run risks. I could be wrong, you know.'

'Not you. Where would I be without your second sight?'

'You don't need it. You can now make your own good fortune. I worried a bit over Guy, although I liked him very much, and wondered if your mother would strip you of your energy and humour. They were both selfish people but Paul is your salvation and he'll be like a rock for you and your family.'

'I know.' Emma turned away, her eyes damp, and when she turned back Emily was busy sorting oranges in the fruit bowl. Family? Emma thought. I have my family. Paul and Rose are enough, aren't they? We are complete.

As if she had heard Emma's unspoken thoughts, Emily looked at her with a gentle expression, the fruit spread over the tablecloth and the one 'specky' orange she had found set aside on a plate. 'Rose isn't enough,' she said. 'Don't leave it too long or she'll lack something she needs, and so will Paul.'

Nine

'We *are* going for several weeks,' Emma said when Paul looked aghast at the number of cases lying ready to be packed.

'There are such things as dry cleaners and laundries,' he said mildly.

'There will be so many different places where we'll need clothes to suit the occasion. Bea said, in her new American phraseology, that we have already been invited to some very prestigious tables in Washington and Dwight wants us to go to the main American Air Force base near Boston when you go there for the Harvard lecture tour. I remember the wonderful clothes and make-up the women wore when they came to England and we had parties with Bea's godfather, the General. We had to try very hard to keep up with them when clothes were rationed.' She laughed. 'The men looked good too, so you must pack an outfit for every occasion.' She kissed him and ruffled his hair. 'You are so good-looking that I shall be very proud to be seen with you whatever you wear.'

'I refuse to wear a checked backwoodsman shirt and go duck shooting.'

'What about ice skating? Bea is very keen just now.'

'No ice skating and no barn dancing.'

'Spoilsport. Nobody has suggested that.'

'It's only a matter of time,' he replied darkly. 'I'm beginning to distrust all things American and our dear Bea Miller in particular.'

Emma giggled. 'She's so excited and she wants us to see and do just about every-thing.'

'Crikey!' Mick's head appeared round the door. 'You really are leaving.'

'Anything urgent?'

'No, Doc. Just that Eileen said that she's making the tea and there's hot apple cake waiting in the kitchen. Oh, yes...'

'What is it?'

'What's-his-name Allen rang. Would you believe he wants you to give him a reference

182

to begin a course in psychology at the Tech. Doesn't give up, does he? I referred him to the probation officer as they said we must if he contacted us when he didn't go to chokey for impersonating a medic.'

Paul sighed. 'If he rings again I'm afraid he's Dr Forsyth's headache now.'

'No need. I sorted him out, Doc, and he sounded as if he took the hint at last but he hates having to report to the probation officer.'

'I feel rather sorry for him and I hope they follow up his case and give him psychiatric help. He does have a certain ability but not enough, as two medical schools found out. With his vanity and ambition he could do a great deal of damage if he worked without proper training. I no longer feel responsible for him and I still have work to do before we leave, but Dr Forsyth seems to have everything under control as far as the clinic here is concerned and I know that you will tie up any loose ends, Mick.'

'I finished the case histories and included the notes you left with them. I thought you might need more than one copy in case you lose them or are robbed in Central Park or down some dark alley, so I made three carbons.'

'I think you ought to come with us,' Paul said.

'Not on your Nellie. I've had enough of overseas and Eileen would kill me.'

'Why does everyone try to frighten us about America? Bea has never had trouble and Dwight thinks that New York is safer than London or Paris.'

'You aren't going to New York,' Mick said cryptically as if the rest of America was very dangerous. 'Eileen made me get rid of my old gun or you could have that.'

'No guns!' Paul said firmly. 'Come on, I can smell apple cake.'

'If Eileen feeds me like this I shall be one obese psychiatrist by the time you come back. How do you manage to stay so slim, Paul?' Robert Forsyth took his plate over near the fire.

'Self-discipline,' Paul said, taking a large slice of apple cake. 'I'll have to stay slim. My darling wife has crazy ideas about what the modern man is wearing in the States. What is more, she has already bought me some clothes and I suppose I have to wear them.'

'Such as?'

'Coloured silk waistcoats to wear under dark suits, a silk umbrella because my old brolly is splitting at the seams and a bowler hat to impress our ex-colonials.'

Robert choked on a crumb. 'I thought we were entering an era of freedom where men never wear hats and they are allowed to have hairy tweeds and yellow ties with foxes all over them.'

'They are there too, for the country, complete with leather patches on the elbows.'

Emma feigned indignance. 'I bought those because Bea wanted some for Dwight who fancies himself as a country squire or whatever they call them over there. She thinks it might make him spend some time in Texas at the family ranch, but he seems tied to Washington and the White House staff, sometimes in uniform and sometimes in formal office clothes.'

'It was easier when we had clothes rationing. I had the choice of one good dark suit from pre-war days and a series of sweaters hand-knitted by aunts and grateful patients and a blazer passed down from my father. Now I have three suits and can never decide what to wear,' Robert said. He laughed. 'I don't envy you, Paul. When do we see you with a Tony Curtis hair cut?'

'On the day you see me with a shoelace necktie and velvet lapels on my jackets. I am rapidly trying to find excuses to stay here. We even bought some Frankie Laine records for Bea and a terrible one of Johnny Ray where he cries as soon as the song gets a bit sentimental.'

Eileen was cutting apple cake to take down to her own quarters. 'Johnny Ray is lovely,' she said as if defending a dear friend. 'I cry too when he starts and it's really moving. He's so sincere.'

Emma took a cream-coloured raincoat from a hanger by the fire and shook it briskly. 'This seemed like a good idea in the shop. Everyone is wearing belted raincoats with rubberised linings but they do smell at first and I am hoping that a warm kitchen will take away the smell before Paul wears it.'

'Yes, the smell of rubber in a warm room isn't very good. I'd rather it smelled of roast beef or chocolate cake,' Paul decided. 'I hope it doesn't attract more odours or I'll have all the dogs in Washington following me.' He tried it on. 'Isn't it a bit on the military side for me, a dedicated civilian?'

'Fashion still says uniforms and broad shoulders,' Robert assured him. 'I suppose that the lads now doing National Service are used to wearing uniform and may even like the trend. I think we shall see clothes like this for years in the future, unless the Edwardian influence catches on with the general public and not just with the few rebels who want to be different.'

Emma consulted a list. 'I have a few more bits and pieces to buy for Bea. She wants school blazers for the twins. I did ask if she was serious and she said that when the children have to go with her and Dwight to meet important people she wants them to look very smart and very British. Besides, blazers are very useful at any time, but even Bea draws the line at the type of caps that boys wear at school here.'

'There's still a lot to do and I seem to be making new lists all the time to make sure everything runs smoothly for Robert and Mick,' Paul sighed.

'When I was in America visiting my uncle, we were treated to every luxury possible,' Emma said. 'I tried to think of something that we didn't have there that I could take over for Bea. Not easy as they seem to have everything but I remembered that one morning I asked for a boiled egg for breakfast and it came sliding about already shelled in a small dish with a spoon but no egg cup. The waiter didn't know what I wanted when I asked for an egg cup and from his expression he thought I was a very strange female, so I've bought half a dozen china egg cups to take over with us. It will be a talking point if nothing else.'

Rose was given a small attaché-case to pack a selection of her favourite toys and soon the nursery was strewn with everything from her toy box and the case was already full to overflowing. Emma left her, as she was absorbed, but decided that the case would not be packed until the evening before their departure and the lid could be closed when Rose was asleep.

As the day of their leaving drew near, the telephone rang incessantly as more and more of their friends heard of the lecture tours and those who had met Bea wanted to send their regards.

'He insists,' Miranda said, when Paul tried to refuse her husband's offer of a huge limousine to take them all to the docks. 'Don't say no as he really wants to help and wishes he could come with us on the *Queen Mary* but he will come with us to the ship and see me installed safely. He fusses over me as if I might break in the middle,' she added happily. 'We shall need that car, with all our luggage, and we might have to be followed by another smaller car with the excess. I took a look at my cases and I can't believe that I have so many clothes! I couldn't travel by air. They'd forbid me to take all that on a plane.'

'Have you everything you need for your injections?' Emma asked her.

'My own doctor has been in touch with the shipping office and we shall be able to use their sick bay for sterilising the syringes and giving the injections. Once I am in the States my dresser will cope with all that as she will have a small electric steriliser with her and all the testing equipment. She is a gem and did a lot of VAD work at the end of the war so I trust her implicitly.'

'We'll be ready for the driver to collect our luggage in plenty of time to embark at Southampton.' Emma told them. 'If we are early, we can see the docks from the ship and listen to the band they have there to send off the liners going to America or South Africa. I've told Rose that we can take coloured paper streamers to throw from the ship and she is enchanted as she is not allowed to spread bits of paper around the house!'

'Emily was a bit too generous,' Paul said dryly, 'but I suppose we'll have to take every one of the dozen packets of streamers. I asked where she bought them and she told me about the local annual carnivals they have on the island, where streamers are a part of each parade.'

'I remember them,' Emma said dreamily.

'The red ones were my favourites, but I was allowed only one packet. A lot of my school friends saved theirs and had fights with them in the recreation field and were told off about the mess, but I used all mine to throw at the various floats and wagons.'

'I must have had a very deprived childhood,' Paul said, and his smile was teasing. 'I love you when you go all soft about the past. I wish that I had been brought up in a smaller community. I think you had more fun than I did.'

'The summer visitors made a difference. The town councils arranged fêtes and carnivals to attract money to the island and we were a part of it as we belonged to a sports club and the Girl Guides. I was a flower fairy, shivering in a paper dress on one float and another year I was a Dutch girl on the wagon decorated with artificial tulips. I bought a pair of wooden clogs for that but didn't realise that we had to walk in procession in the main arena. My feet were covered with blisters after that and I never wore them again.'

'What it is to be a star.'

Emma gave her husband a dirty look. 'I suffered!'

'It sounds lovely.' Eileen sighed. 'I can just imagine my Jean as a fairy.'

'She could be if you take a holiday with my aunt on the island next year in the middle of August. She has invited you, I know, and maybe even Mick could be persuaded to go then. Jean would be too young to enjoy it this year, but next year would be fun as she would be old enough for the junior parade they have one afternoon during the carnival.'

'Meanwhile,' Paul interrupted, 'there is a little matter of America on which to concentrate our thoughts. That is if you are not planning to be a majorette over there. Do you realise that we leave tomorrow?'

'I'd drop the batons,' Emma chuckled. 'You are quite safe. I have no more ambitions to cavort about in fancy dress, and we are all packed up ready to go.'

'You asked me to hide the big bear,' Eileen said. 'Rose saw me put it in the cupboard and she pulled it out at once and has played with it ever since. Sorry about that.'

'We can't take that huge thing with us,' Paul asserted. 'I think that Teddy is about to have a nasty accident.'

'And have your daughter needing a psychiatrist?' Emma laughed. 'I'll let her make pastry. The birds will have bent beaks when I tip it out but that's their worry.'

'I'm getting good at pretending to eat her masterpieces,' Paul said. 'I found a large lump of iron-hard stuff in the pocket of a coat I put out for cleaning last week.'

'While she's busy I'll take the bear down to our flat,' Eileen promised. 'Now that the weather is fine I'll take her out to the park with Jean and that will tire her out tonight.'

'Good. We have an early start tomorrow and we need her to be wide awake when we get to Southampton.'

It was strange to think that they wouldn't see the house or the practice in Kensington for a very long time and Emma had last minute misgivings. Suppose she hated America? Suppose Paul worked too hard there and gave in to far too many requests for his time and expertise? Suppose she found that Bea had altered and was now a stranger?

'Cold feet?' Paul asked when they were ready for bed.

She smiled wanly. 'I don't think I need a hot-water bottle.'

'That could be remedied easily, but you do look a little fraught.'

'Just a little.'

'I feel the same.'

'But you are so calm and organised!'

'Not inside. I see dragons round every American corner and I know they'll hate me!'

'They'll love you almost as much as I do. I do love you, Paul.'

He held her close and caressed her in the way she needed to be touched, and made love gently. 'That's all that matters,' he murmured. 'The next time we make love we will be far away in a strange country.'

'But we shall be together,' she said, softly.

As if she knew that something very exciting was happening, Rose pulled Paul's hair to wake him up at six the next morning. Emma was wide awake and had crept into the kitchen to make tea. All three of them sat on the bed, Rose with a beaker of orange juice and Paul holding the hot mug of tea between both his hands. Emma looked yet again at her list of last minute things to do and sighed.

'I know I have forgotten something but I have given up trying to think.'

'I've packed,' Rose said loftily.

'Your case is down with the others,' Paul assured her, hoping that she wouldn't want one last inspection of her case of toys.

'And you have a new coat to wear,' Emma reminded her.

By the time the car arrived, with Miranda and her husband seated in the back and an alarming number of suitcases in the boot, Emma was dressed in a new suit with a pulled in waist and padded shoulders and a silk scarf that filled the neckline but made no bulk under the close-fitting bodice. Her high heels and sheer silk stockings made her seem tall and slim and her leather handbag was the same tobacco brown of the shoes.

'You all look lovely,' Eileen said with satisfaction. 'Give my love to Mrs Miller and himself and a kiss for the children.'

Emma's eyes were moist and she found it difficult to say goodbye. Even Mick's voice was husky and abrupt as they packed the luggage into the car and onto a large roof rack. They turned away from the house where they were all so happy and wondered why they were foolish enough to want to leave, even when they knew they would return.

As the car drew away from the drive, Emma had a sense of déjà vu. When she had left home for the hospital where she was to train, she had felt she was free, but when she returned on holiday, leaving her work and friends behind her, she had felt a sense of dread because she was going to be with her demanding mother again. Now, she just felt a dull ache. She glanced at Paul's set face and knew he was having the same experience. Miranda on the other hand was bubbling over with excitement, and her husband smiled indulgently as she prattled on about the wonderful letters she'd received from her agent and producer in America.

'I'm so glad you are going to be with my

wife,' he said. 'Give my love to Bea and tell her that I will try to come over quite soon as I have to see a minister in the White House and can make it coincide with Miranda's debut into the American theatre.'

Southampton was bright and the sun shone on the huge liners in the various docks, as if, finally, all traces of war and privation had been thrust away and there was an uplift to life; only a few empty shells of buildings gave a hint of what had happened in the war years. At last, Emma felt a rising excitement, and Rose couldn't sit still.

'Look Rose! That's the ship we shall be in tonight,' she pointed out and suddenly the *Queen Mary* seemed almost too big to be real.

The luggage was seized by an army of skilled handlers and disappeared into the dark interior while passengers walked up the sloping gangways to be greeted by the ship's personnel and escorted to their cabins.

Although Miranda was travelling incognito, one or two people nudged each other as they recognised her and Paul wondered if she would be allowed to remain just Lady Shuter and not the glamorous actress who had made such a success of her career in the West End of London.

Once on board they heard the music from a Guards' band and found their way to the ship's side overlooking the dock. Uniforms of red and black with fur-trimmed cockaded hats made a patch of colour against the grey stones, and the silver trumpets gleamed in the sunlight. Tunes from popular musicals hung on the air and the engines of the huge ship began to throb into life.

Rose wanted to sit on the rail but Paul held her firmly and she was soon absorbed by the sights on the shore, the sounds of music, and the seemingly never-ending trail of passengers coming on board.

A siren gave a signal that the ship would leave shortly and a voice over a loudhailer called, 'ALL ASHORE WHO'S GOING ASHORE. ALL PASSENGERS ON BOARD. ALL VISITORS LEAVE NOW. ALL ASHORE WHO'S GOING ASHORE.'

Miranda clung to her husband for a minute; he kissed Emma and Rose, shook Paul's hand and hastily left the deck, his face showing deep emotion, as if the temporary parting was too poignant to prolong.

The atmosphere must have been like this when troops left for foreign waters and the unknown, Emma thought, but then there would not have been coloured streamers to lighten the leaving. It was electric and exciting but somehow sad. The band struck up again. 'Will ye no come back again?' and tears began to fall as coloured streamers were unrolled into the air and the thin bands of colour flew in wide arches to beribbon the sides of the vessel and land on the quay. Rose was enchanted and threw her streamers, some unfolding and some leaving her small hands still in tight rolls, but her face was alive with wonder as the rainbow of colour became a dense cloud of farewell.

The hawsers were stowed and the vessel left the moorings; the streamers broke as they were pulled from the shore and the symbolic severing of contact was complete.

The *Queen Mary*, now pushed by fussy

tugs, was pointed in the direction of the open Southampton Water, the Needles on the Isle of Wight, and then the wide open sea, towards America; the ragged remains of the streamers were torn away in the wind as if the passengers had indeed severed all contacts with home.

Ten

Emma rang for the steward and asked to be shown where the ship's sick bay was situated. She regarded Miranda with some anxiety as she looked flushed and overexcited. 'It's time for your evening injection,' she pointed out.

'I'm not really hungry.' Miranda said firmly. 'I could miss this one and not eat this evening.'

'You know better than that,' Emma replied, and although Paul said nothing, Miranda sensed his disapproval, lowered her gaze and shrugged. 'You really do intend to make me be good. You are right, of course, and it's nice to know you care enough to bully me.'

'Come on, the steward is waiting, and this isn't going to take long.' Emma picked up the case containing all the equipment that Miranda needed for injections and urine testing for her condition.

The small clinical room was well equipped and Emma looked about her with approval and interest. Only a faint humming from the distant engines, and the small round porthole windows, made it apparent that this was not on land. A nursing sister greeted them with a welcoming smile and was obviously impressed by the fact that a very famous and beautiful star of a long-running play on the stage, and soon possibly of the screen, was in her domain.

She took the specimen of urine that Miranda produced and tested it for sugar and acetone, then charted a drop of blood to start a blood sugar curve as an extra precaution in case Miranda was careless in her diet. The atmosphere of the room, smelling of disinfectant, calmed her and when they returned to the suite, Miranda was relaxed and said she thought she could manage dinner.

'We'll eat here tonight,' Paul insisted, then added, as if to make sure that Miranda didn't feel that she was the only one to be considered, 'Rose is overtired and I don't want to leave her with a stranger tonight while we are in the dining-room.'

'That's good. I don't want to have people staring at me and wondering if I am who I am,' Miranda agreed. She examined her reflection in one of the mirrors in the suite. 'I feel a bit tired but I certainly don't look it.' She stared at herself in the mirror. 'I'm amazed at how well I look.'

Paul walked over to stand behind her and smiled above her head into the mirror. He laughed and Miranda turned to look at him then back at the mirror. 'I think we should have a looking-glass like this in our clinic,' he said. 'Very flattering and good for the morale. Patients would go home convinced that they were very much better just because they saw their faces in a flattering reflection when they tidied hair and fixed make-up before leaving the clinic.'

Miranda put a hand up to the glass, then smiled. 'What a mean trick. We all look better in this mirror and I can see now that the glass is tinted peachy pink. What a good thing I brought a glass that shows up every blemish. I couldn't face the photographers, believing that I looked this good after seeing myself in this peachy glow. The camera they say never lies but I would blame the photographer if I appeared badly on film after putting on my make-up in this mirror.'

The suite of rooms was spacious and well appointed with solid and handsome furniture and pastel shades over the small lamps dotted about in useful positions by the inviting deep armchairs. Rose made no fuss about sleeping in a tiny room with a porthole window. Her favourite toys were scattered on the floor and she hugged a smaller version of her bear.

A handwritten invitation came for Miranda and her party to dine at the captain's table. She pleaded exhaustion but told the messenger that they would be pleased to accept the invitation for the following night.

'We are on our way,' Emma whispered, as they prepared for bed after a wonderful meal brought into the suite on a wide trolley that doubled as a table. Suddenly, she was very tired, the tension of the past few days catching up with her.

Paul yawned. 'Tonight I shall hear nothing but the sea and the distant engines, if I hear a thing,' and they were fast asleep when the steward brought early morning tea and the ship's newspaper with details of all the activities available for passengers energetic enough to sample them, and details of the daily gamble over the speed of the ship that day and the sea miles covered.

In a simple beige trouser suit and dark glasses, Miranda was sufficiently unrecognisable to venture into the dining-room for breakfast after being given her first injection of the day and she read for a while on a recliner on the promenade deck while Emma and Paul took Rose to explore the ship.

Slightly overawed by the immense funnels and the wake of white foam that thundered after the ship, Rose was quiet and content to walk with her parents, Paul's hand held tightly in hers for reassurance, but later, she was persuaded to join several other children in a nursery filled with toys and exercise equipment, including a rocking horse, and Emma was free to enjoy the ambience of the voyage.

It was strange, after a lifetime of caring for others and working so hard, to be at leisure, on call to nobody except Miranda – who was little trouble – and every wish immediately granted, or in some cases, anticipated. Hot bouillon appeared when they joined Miranda to sit on the deck recliners and she was able to drink some as it was safely free of carbohydrate, but stimulated her appetite for lunch.

'I needed this time away from everything,' she said and sighed with contentment.

'I think we all needed a break,' Paul agreed. 'After this I shall be ready for work again, but it will be nothing so taxing as life in the clinic in London.'

The steward took away the evening dresses and Paul's dress suit for pressing and Emma was free to do as she liked all day. Rose was very busy with her new friends and Paul took pleasure in walking the decks and exploring the ship's library. They dressed for dinner early as they had been invited to a cocktail party before they ate at the captain's table, and Emma was impressed by the almost pre-war elegance of the guests and the magnificence of the cut glass and ancient silver in the dining-room.

It was hard to imagine the ship divested of all that luxury, and stripped of everything moveable that could be stowed safely during the war and not brought out again until it was safe to display them again. She tried to visualise the public rooms filled with iron bedsteads and bunks to accommodate thousands of soldiers during the war. The *Queen Mary* had not sailed the Atlantic proudly, as a queen of the sea, but had been forced to take avoiding actions and steer devious courses when enemy submarines were suspected to be within range with torpedoes.

Emma looked about her and wondered if all that drabness could ever have existed, and after dinner sat in a comfortable plush-covered chair to listen to a concert of light music, played by a well-known dance band that she had previously heard only on the wireless.

The four days passed in a kind of indulgent dream and Miranda valued the private suite. Having appeared at dinner with the captain and other important people, Miranda was unable to remain incognito. At dinner, she was beautiful, dressed in a slim, silk dress and high-heeled sandals, her skin radiant and her hair loose as she wore it in the latest play. In the suite, she could relax and avoid the few pushy fans who tried to dog her steps. Emma and Paul kept a protective eye on her and she made full use of the hairdresser, the beautician and the Swiss masseuse on board.

Refreshed and bright-eyed, they packed ready for disembarkation; Rose said a tearful goodbye to the nursery nurse and the little girl who by now was her very best friend in all the world, and Miranda posed for the press and photographers.

On deck as the great ship eased her way into New York Harbour, the passengers crowded the rails to catch the first glimpse of the Statue of Liberty. Emma was overwhelmed by the dignity, style and impressive size of the famous edifice and many of the passengers had tears in their eyes when they saw it for the first time or felt they were returning home to familiar sights after being abroad.

Gulls wheeled above *Queen Mary's* funnels, and sirens from the shore and the many tugs easing her into harbour made her arrival an occasion for welcome and anticipation. The smartly uniformed pilots were piped aboard at the harbour entrance as soon as the ship's speed reduced, and eventually the docking was made fast, as the hawsers were tied to the quay side.

Music from a brass band was as bright and foot-tapping as the music at American forces' dances in London, Emma recalled, and the irreverent strains of 'The American Patrol' belted out over the sea. Paul grinned. 'Now I really believe I am in America.'

Everything was well organised. Miranda was greeted by her dresser, Doreen Birch, and Emma passed over the diabetic equipment that she'd used on board. 'I shall see you when we come to Washington,' Miranda said and kissed Emma with real affection.

'I have a car waiting, Lady Shuter,' Doreen said, then conceded, 'you look really well,' as if she expected the worst when her charge was out of her vigilance for five minutes. The slightly angular, plain woman was obviously fond of Miranda and scooped her back into her care as soon as the luggage had been taken to the car. 'You'll have a rest as soon as we get there. I've arranged it, and a little light lunch, but I made it clear that you would not want to meet any friends that your hostess has invited to meet you until you have recovered from the voyage, and then only those who were connected with the theatre,' Doreen said firmly. She sniffed dismissively. 'Social climbers! They are as bad here as they are in London although they boast that America has no class system.'

Paul exchanged amused glances with his wife and wondered if Doreen had taken over the whole of their hostess's house. He decided that in any argument Doreen would come out victorious and would protect Miranda's interests beyond the call of duty.

When she hugged Emma, Miranda whispered, 'She bullies everyone including me but she's quite indispensable and I love her.'

A limousine took the Sykes family smoothly to the airport after they passed through immigration, and a small executive plane, gleaming and new, was waiting on the tarmac.

'Is this an Air Force plane?' asked Paul.

'Seconded to Mr Miller,' the steward told him. 'In fact it is for the private use of Mr Miller and his party and a few other diplomats and senators. Champagne, Mrs Sykes?'

Paul raised his eyebrows. 'Dwight must be really important,' he said.

'I hope not *too* important,' Emma remarked. 'I remember him as a fairly simple man whom we all loved.'

'He hasn't changed,' Paul said warmly. 'When I speak to him on the phone he sounds just as we remember him.'

'That's the private man,' Emma remarked shrewdly. 'He must be very disciplined and more formal in his work and we have never seen Dwight Miller, the diplomat.'

'With Bea as his wife, he would never have a chance to be pompous and overbearing as some important people become. Remember

Dwight with a clothes-peg on his nose, changing a nappy? Bea stood over him and told him that if he didn't want to do it, he should never have been so potent as to sire twins.'

'Dear Bea, that was when his morale needed a boost after he thought he might be unable to give her babies. She took every opportunity to make him believe that he was very important and virile.' Emma giggled. 'After the next baby was born, Bea decided that enough was enough and told me that she'd said 'Whoops, down boy!' and gone back to wearing a diaphragm.'

A late lunch was served during the flight to Washington and once again, Emma was intrigued by the imaginative presentation of American food but thought that Aunt Emily would turn her nose up at the bland flavour. Prawns from the warm waters of the Pacific had the texture of cotton wool and were rather tasteless. She could smell no hint of the sea like the shellfish off Bembridge on the Isle of Wight and those from cooler northern waters, when served on ice.

'Don't say it!' Paul cautioned. 'You are in

enemy territory and we like everything we are offered,' he added, as if reading her thoughts.

'I hope that Rose is as tactful.' The remains of a discarded creamy dessert of bright pink with curls of chocolate and a badly chewed cookie showed that Rose had not as yet been converted to what she saw as strange foreign food. Everything looked appetising and Rose was a greedy little girl but as Aunt Emily's Wilf would say when anyone left food, 'Your eyes were bigger than your belly!'

The long distance between New York and Washington made Emma aware of the immense size of the country and she knew that they would not be able to see even a fraction of it, but the important thing was that she was going to see Bea Miller, the girl who would always be her spiritual sister after all they had shared during hospital training: sadness, anxiety and great joy. She smiled and the corners of her mouth trembled. Paul held her hand. 'Happy?'

'I can hardly believe it.' Emma glanced at Rose who was busily drawing an aeroplane to show Dwight. 'He'll like that. I don't suppose he's ever flown in one quite like it,' she said, observing the peculiar set of the wings.

'I think the pilot might need a parachute,' Paul whispered but promised to fold the paper carefully and carry it in his pocket, ready to give to Dwight.

The exclusive area of the airport away from the main terminal was reserved for government planes, diplomats and high ranking service personnel. It was bare except for two small planes similar to the one in which they had just flown, but from the main runways came the sounds of sirens, heavy engines and the swish of luggage vehicles.

Paul looked out of the window as their plane taxied to a halt. 'There they are!' He was as excited as Emma and picked up Rose, ready to leave the plane at the first possible moment.

Bea stood by a large limousine, looking relaxed and nonchalant as if it was an everyday occurrence to greet her friend from England after such a long time away from each other. As usual she was dressed in elegant clothes and her blonde hair, now shorter than Emma recalled, was as smooth and shining as burnished white gold against the dark blue coat and multicoloured scarf. At Beatties Bea had had a reputation for appearing aloof, and she appeared so now, until Emma put her foot on American soil and ran forward.

The cool illusion vanished and Bea rushed to meet her with tears running down her cheeks. 'About time! What kept you?' They hugged and Paul felt a lump in his throat as he greeted Dwight.

'Paul! You are handsomer than ever,' Bea said and was kissed with great enthusiasm.

'You limeys! Emma and I will get on fine if you have to keep on hugging each other. I think she's prettier than you, Bea.' Dwight kissed Emma and stood with an arm around her shoulders. She sensed his genuine pleasure and they all started to talk, stopped and then interrupted each other as words tumbled out in an unintelligible tangle of excitement.

'Take no notice of my husband,' Bea

warned Emma. 'He is too big for his boots these days. I hope you didn't pack any presents for him. Don't encourage him.'

'No children?' asked Emma. Rose was looking about her and walked over to the motor car to see if they were inside.

'We left them back home so that we could have a little conversation without them hogging your attention,' Dwight said. 'Gee, it's good to see you,' he repeated for the third time. 'Now I can get Bea off my back. Right up to yesterday she worried in case you didn't come.'

'You didn't get excited, I suppose,' Bea retorted. 'Who rang the chauffeur twice to make sure the car was 100 per cent ready?'

'That's not just any old car, and I wanted to drive it today,' Dwight said and Paul inspected the huge Cadillac. 'It isn't one of the official fleet. I've begun collecting vintage cars. This is my best so far and belonged to Douglas Fairbanks, but what I really want is a Silver Ghost Rolls Royce and an early Bugatti.'

Bea smiled. 'Fairly innocuous, but expensive,' she said. 'A lot of sugary sentimentality that does nobody any harm. I've a better feeling about it than the one we went around in during the war,' she added softly. 'Remember the terrible car with curtains and soft cushions that was a passion wagon belonging to that assassin Goering? I wished that the boys had never 'liberated' it. I hated it and could imagine shocking things happening in it and not all were to do with sex.'

'If you are determined to go down memory lane take another turning,' Paul advised them.

'Quite right,' Dwight agreed piously. 'Keep Bea off the war. She swears she never talks about it but as soon as some brainless idiot with more fat on his butt than sense, mentions how he did very well out of munitions or food supplies to the Allies, she loses her cool and tells him a thing or two that he doesn't want to know. They'll deport her one day,' he added cheerfully.

In the car, Bea took Rose on her knee and pointed out another little girl with two dogs on leads in a park bordering the wide road. 'I want a puppy,' Rose said, and Emma wondered if a dog would be an adequate substitute for another baby.

'We have a dog,' Bea told her. 'We are lucky to live outside the city where there is space for dogs but you are surrounded by houses and busy roads in London so it would not be easy to cope with a puppy.'

'Does your dog bite?' Rose wanted to know. 'What's his name?'

'He only bites his dinner and dog biscuits,' Dwight said. 'He licks a lot and likes little girls. He's a spaniel with floppy ears and a waggy tail.'

The few miles of well-washed streets and fine buildings gave way to a more gentle scene with avenues of shady trees and warm red-brick edges to the grass verges. A party of children on ponies, led by a woman in smart riding breeches and a well-cut jacket, made slow progress along the road ahead and drew closer to the verge as the car passed them. Bea waved and the woman saluted with her riding crop.

'Do you know her?' asked Emma, and Rose stared wide-eyed at the disappearing procession.

'She gives lessons to the children, and they are really keen to learn. Her stables are quite close to our house and we can take Rose along to look at the horses later.'

'Rose has only sat on a donkey a couple of times when we went to the island to see Aunt Emily. Wilf keeps one in his field to keep down the thistles and he's amiable and slow, which is wonderful for small children.'

'A small pony on a leading rein will give her confidence,' Bea suggested and laughed. 'It's a wonderful time-consuming pastime and children do get very absorbed with riding and everything to do with horses.'

The one-storey house sprawled across a wide patio and looked out onto a very English-looking lawn, with flower-beds and a hedge that separated the garden from an orchard and a vegetable garden. A glass conservatory with a raised ridge of Victorian wrought iron on the roof was full of leafy plants and garden furniture. A gardener straightened his back to watch the party go into the house.

The cool blues and greens of the window drapes in the main sitting-room and the spare use of furniture was refreshing and attractive, but Bea took them along a corridor to a small suite of rooms that she explained would be for their use all the time they were in America.

'Not that you will be here much during the day. We have so much to do and many people want to meet you. The children can play in their own nursery, and thank God for good nannies.'

'We'll fit in with any plans you have and make ourselves scarce when you have official visitors,' Paul said. 'I'll let you have details of my own itinerary which will take a lot of my time, but I hope we can do a lot together.'

Eleven

'Oh, there you are. I think she's still asleep so be quiet, children!' Emma opened her eyes and saw three solemn faces staring at her over the bed rail. The voice behind them was soft and the dark face laughing. 'I'm sorry if they woke you, Madam, but they have been awake for hours, wanting to see you, and they escaped me.'

Emma struggled into her dressing gown and swung her legs over the side of the bed. 'I'm awake,' she said and smiled. 'Hello, you three, where's Rose?'

'Dr Sykes took her to see the garden and the fish pool. I'm Ellie and I look after the children for breakfast when they've had their baths, while Mrs Miller gets herself set for the day and writes letters.'

'We wanted to see you,' Johnny said and Avril nodded vigorously.

'I want to play with Rose,' Mark added.

221

'Later, Honey,' Ellie laughed. 'Yesterday he fell in the fish pool and Mrs Miller said he must stay away from that part of the garden for three days.'

'Mark likes water,' Avril said. 'He dunks himself in any he can find and Mother gets mad at him.'

'Leave Mrs Sykes to get dressed and we'll go find Rose for breakfast. Mr Miller had to go out early but you and your husband and Mrs Miller can have your breakfast in peace on the terrace.'

The children left with Ellie, and Emma was impressed by their acceptance of what they were told. They were lightly disciplined but obviously not repressed. Emma laughed softly. Bea had not lost her touch. Strong men had obeyed her slightest order and there had seldom been a time when she was confronted by mutiny from any of the patients on her wards of orthopaedic Army casualties at Heath Cross and Beatties.

The suite of rooms was neat and pretty, with just enough muted elegance to show the care that had been taken with the decor. Expensive without opulence, Emma decided, and luxuriated in the shell-pink shower room and the huge matching towels and bath soap.

'You conscious, Sister Dewar?'

Emma draped herself in a bath towel and brushed the damp hair from her eyes. 'Quite decent and almost human.'

'I hope you like American breakfasts?' Bea was cool and immaculate in a shirtwaister dress of soft yellow with gold buttons and a simple chain at her throat.

'Not dieting?' asked Emma.

'Never!' Bea twirled to show her slim hips and trim bustline. 'I have far too much to do to put on weight. The kids keep me like this and wear me ragged.' She sat on the bed while Emma dressed. She eyed the full navy blue skirt and pale blue blouse with amusement. 'Almost a uniform, but nice,' she announced. 'I suppose you really do work in the clinic, and it shows. All you need with that skirt is a wide blue belt with a silver buckle and then you'd really look like a Beattie's Sister.' She laughed. 'We'll soon change all that. This morning we show Rose the horses and maybe sit her on a fat old pony we keep for timid visitors. It's useful having a stable close by where we can leave our own horses and have them to ride whenever we want them, but we let Eve, who owns the stables, use them when we are away. That pays for their keep and exercises them.' Bea sighed. 'I'm really happy here but I wish we had more time to visit Texas and let the children ride in a more free atmosphere. Here we trot along established bridle paths and along the side of the exercise field and it's a bit like riding in Rotten Row, at home.'

'They really enjoy horses?'

'Love them, but Mark is a little bit of a trial as he makes them canter when we are in a zone reserved for more sober riding. He's adventurous like his father.'

'Who are the twins like?'

'A mixture. Avril looks like me, thank God, and not Dwight's sister who is a bit butch, and Johnnie is like Dwight with a bit of my father thrown in. Mark will be a tearaway or a film stuntman, or maybe a future President of the US of A, or an explorer.'

Emma laughed. 'From what Ellie said, he might even be a deep-sea diver.'

'Ellie does the early stint and hands over to the nanny at ten. She gives them small jobs to do and makes them read for half an hour, mostly English favourites and less of the *Little Black Sambo* and *Uncle Remus* kind of books. Stop looking quizzical, Dewar. I take care to give them the best of both countries, with no prejudice, and if I lived in a country where the local language was foreign to us, they would be bilingual.' She shrugged. 'I sometimes think I'm losing a battle over diction but on the whole they are not terribly Yankie, wouldn't you agree?'

'I think they are wonderful,' Emma said simply.

'C'mon. I'm starving. Paul is on the terrace taking photographs of the house and Rose has deserted you for Mark who she kissed twice as soon as she saw him, little hussy!'

'He should feel honoured. It isn't every boy who gets that treatment.'

'He's going to be like his father,' Bea said dryly, 'but where did Rose get that flirty look? Not from you, and Paul hides his libido under that wonderful sexy calm. Do all his female patients fall in love with him?'

'I keep him well chaperoned but you should see the malicious glances I get when I sit in with him on analysis sessions. They make every excuse to get me out of the room, so I send in Mick who can sort out threats from both sexes.'

'Both sexes?' Bea giggled. 'For a man like Paul the odd queer must be far more terrifying than an army of nymphos.'

'Giggling already? I should have known that you'd take over where the last bit of conspiracy left off,' Paul said, joining them.

'Only talking about you, Sweetie,' Bea said. 'Take a picture of Emma and me before we get mussed up by the children and then we must introduce you to Hickory-smoked crisp bacon, maple syrup and pancakes.'

Coffee arrived in a silver pot, and dishes covered with silver domes gleamed on the table in a patch of sun on the terrace. In the distance the hum from the expressway made a background reminiscent of the whine of trams from the hill up to the park near Beatties, and yet there were no really intrusive noises.

'We're very lucky to have this house,' Bea told them. 'Masses of rooms for visitors and a staff annexe where Ellie and Nanny and other female staff live, and an apartment for the gardeners and male staff if they want to live in.'

'This is much too relaxing,' Paul said as he poured syrup on another pancake. 'No thanks, I've had enough scrambled eggs and I must make a few phone calls, if that's okay?'

'There's a private line in your apartment and Emma and I can look over the garden unless the children are ready for Eve and the horses.' Bea peered over a clump of bushes. 'The car has arrived and Nanny is putting the kids inside, so we'd better be on our way before World War III breaks out.'

Paul walked with them to the car and was introduced to Jan, the nanny, who had been with Bea for a year and was happy to stay with the Miller family. 'We passed that stable on the way here,' Emma said. 'Surely we could walk there? Even Rose can manage that far.'

For a moment, Bea looked bleak. 'We drive the children everywhere. If we walked, the police would stop us and want to know where we were going and even if they know us, they caution us that it isn't wise to be walking along a public highway even for a couple of hundred yards.'

Jan gave a nervous laugh. 'You get used to it, Mrs Sykes. We are pretty safe living here, with security gates and alarms, but this is an area where a lot of important diplomats and senators hang out and it attracts a few nuts from time to time.'

Bea gave Jan a warning glance. 'I'll tell you more later Emma, but we keep a low profile with the children so no more for now. Let's get to the horses.'

Johnny struggled out of the car to show Emma his new shirt and Bea gave a sigh of resignation. 'I know, it's awful! He chose it and his dear daddy approves and says he looks a real regular little guy, so what can I do?' A smile curved her lips and she hugged him and shooed him back inside the car.

'He'll be fit for a lumberjack and nothing more,' she asserted. 'Try not to think of him as a walking chequer-board and wear dark glasses if you can't take all the colours.'

'I think he's cute,' Jan said warmly, and Emma agreed.

Jan drove the car, after making sure that the children buckled up their seat belts and that the doors were locked from the inside, making Emma aware that this was routine and a serious precaution against, as Jan said softly, 'Being jumped at the lights.'

The field into which Jan turned the car was green and well kept and ringed by high, creosoted fences. The outside world seemed cut off and Emma lost her feeling of form-less apprehension. Timber stables with rough shingles on the roofs and stout open half-doors through which horses of various sizes peered over the locked lower doors gave an immediate impression of the countryside, and memories of the rides on Epsom Downs in England were vividly reflected.

Rose jumped up and down. 'Is there a nice donkey?'

Jan took her by the hand. 'Let's just look at them first,' she said wisely, and when Rose saw a large horse led out for a woman to ride, she clutched the friendly hand and drew back.

'Maybe this one,' Jan said softly and Emma saw a Shetland pony that looked as if its back had bowed under the saddles of many fat little children.

'There are two,' Bea explained. 'Sugar and Spice, and Mark likes to ride Spice, so you can try Sugar and ride with him.' She laughed. 'Now you know why I insisted that you bought cotton trousers for Rose. Avril wears them but the boys have heavier denims like the ranchers wear. They think they are tough guys!'

'He looks easy to ride.' Emma smoothed the shaggy coat and brushed the unruly mane away from the pony's face.

Rose beamed, her cheeks warm with excitement. 'Funny saddle, Mummy.'

'Clever girl to notice. All the saddles are American which is fine for the kids when they need to have confidence, but I think they'll have to learn to ride all over again if they want to ride in England. No armchair saddles there,' Bea told Jan and left her to sit Rose on the padded leather seat and urged her to hold tight to the pommel.

'Better keep a leading rein on for the first time,' Eve smiled. 'Not that he has the energy to run away with her but it's a rule and she must begin the right way.'

'You okay? I'll take Emma to see the tack room and all your trophies. See you all later. Have fun.'

Bea led Emma away. 'It will be good for Rose to be without you for a while and I'd better put you in the picture about Washington.'

'So far, I've been very impressed.'

'I know the house is sensational and all that goes with it. You'll meet some very nice people while you are here and a few that I can't like and would prefer not to meet, but I have to bite back a few caustic remarks and smile at times. Dwight tries to limit such meetings, but you know how it is.'

'In ideal times, as Aunt Emily says, you wouldn't cross the road to give them the time of day. Does it worry you? We had plenty of practice in hospital. I've wanted to slap down a few and so have you, but we knew we couldn't.'

'And sometimes got misunderstood when we made efforts to be pleasant.'

'Saturday nights in Casualty were the worst. I can't believe that you have anything as bad here?'

'Not here, but you saw how careful we are with the children outside the gates. They *are* safe, so don't get anxious. It just means that we take precautions. In cars, always lock the doors from the inside, even if you want to travel short distances and think that nothing can happen. All the motors have childproof locks so that even my little fiddle-fingers, Mark, cannot open a door from the inside.'

Emma regarded her with interest rather than anxiety. 'I suppose many people would consider London unsafe, but we get about freely and have very little to scare us. Is some of this American hysteria?'

'Never say that again. The country is full of ex-service men living on state handouts or nothing, and crime has escalated since Korea. Jan was set on by three men who stole her purse but she was wise and did nothing heroic and they didn't hurt her. The police took notes but they have many such complaints every week and seldom arrest anyone.'

'Not everyone has a car, so how do they manage?'

'The buses are good and cheap and we lend Jan a car if she needs to go into the city. She prefers to live in and sleep at nights,' Bea added dryly. 'If you want to explore Washington, downtown, we'll have a man to drive us. I wear no jewellery in the city and carry only what cash I need for that day.' She gave Emma a bear hug. 'Cheer up, you are safe with us and it's just wonderful to have you here. Let's see who has fallen off what!'

Mark was fighting back the tears. 'Tell me,' Bea said gently as she wiped them away from his dirty cheeks.

'Nasty horse,' he mumbled.

'What did you do to him?'

'Nothing.'

Bea sat back on her heels and inspected the grazed arm. 'Nothing?'

His defiant expression wavered and he grinned. 'I hit him with a stick to make him gallop and he tossed me.'

'He had every right to do that. Spice is a civilised animal and you did wrong, Mark. Go into the house and ask Alice to put something on that graze and then sit out here and wait for the others to finish.'

'I want to ride!'

'You'll ride again when you've learned to treat Spice with respect. You may feed him when the morning session is over. Make a fuss of him and say sorry, but you do not ride again today.'

Mark kicked dirt as he went into the house but obeyed his mother and came back with a clean face and a plaster on the graze. Rose sat sedately on Sugar and the twins trotted along the sides of the field and back to the stables when Eve called them.

'They are very good,' Emma remarked, looking at Mark who bore no resentment against his mother's order.

'They have to be,' Bea said firmly. 'They meet a lot of important people and the Americans love the twins' good manners.

Mark could be a problem when he is older as he has a lot of my bolshie attitudes and hates to be held back. I almost wish he'd been a girl like Rose, but not quite. He's afraid of nobody and I hate to disillusion him and say that many people are not good and he must learn not to speak to strangers, but it's difficult to draw a firm line beyond which he must not go.'

'He's little more than a baby,' protested Emma. 'Rose is very trusting too and I worry about her sometimes but she is never away from me or Eileen for very long and she is shy of complete strangers, so that problem doesn't arise.'

They watched the children hold buckets of pony nuts for the Shetlands and Mark made a fuss of Spice and said he was sorry he hit him. Spice nuzzled his neck and crunched the food, obviously not upset and convinced that he'd applied his own effective brand of punishment.

'Home for milk and cookies.' Jan packed the children into the car and Bea came away from Eve's office, after arranging another ride so that Rose could be included.

By the corner of the main road, Emma noticed four men lounging by a hydrant, watching the passing cars, and she felt uneasy. Bea saw her expression and smiled wryly. 'You'll get as bad as me if you stay here. I try not to condemn every layabout I see but I have to be careful since Jan was attacked. If I had them in a ward I'd get to know them and find out if I could trust them, but here, there is a certain us-and-them feeling which is wrong but necessary.'

'Do they ask for casual jobs?'

'Frequently.' Bea frowned. 'We ask for references when we want to employ someone new and we have an ex-naval overseer who knows what to do if he thinks that a man is unsuitable, and never allows anyone inside the main gates without a pass. Mark loves to watch the passing traffic and the arrival of visitors in flashy cars and Jan has her work cut out making sure he doesn't go near the main gate. The nursery nurse should be with him if the twins are visiting their friends but when he runs down to the gate to see if they are coming back she finds him difficult to catch.' Bea sighed. 'She is a great pudding of a girl and slow moving but she's kind and loves the children, so I suppose I have to put up with one or two faults. You'll meet her tomorrow when she comes back from a few days off.'

'While Rose is here Mark will have someone of his own age to play with, and that may make him more amenable.' Emma watched the two youngest children laughing together. 'They get on so well!'

'She could be very good for him,' Bea admitted. 'I'd hate to pin him down too much but he does need to learn self-discipline, even at his age. Never too early for the influence of a good woman! What am I saying? I'll be planning their wedding soon!'

'Don't!' Emma shook her head, laughing. 'They need to go to school before that.'

'I know.' Bea regarded her son with wry affection. 'What do they have in store for us, Dewar?'

Emma glanced at her sharply. Bea called her Dewar less and less and only when she felt something deeply. 'With you as parents, none of them can be bad. I see normal healthy tots who are a credit to your up-bringing and love. It shows Bea, and Dwight is very proud of his family.'

'What does Aunt Emily say about them?'

'Not much. She loved seeing the twins when you brought them over but she hasn't seen Mark. No shadows in her mind about the twins but she laughed at some of the things you say about Mark on the phone and says he needs watching. That's nothing bad,' she added hastily. 'We all gather that he is the active one with too much imagina-tion.' She saw Bea relax and changed the subject. 'Talking of weddings, I have to buy a present for George and his bride. I thought we could find something over here. Any ideas?'

'Something that Margaret will love and yet not be so personal that George will treasure it and think it's for him?'

'Something like that. Something imper-sonal for the home.'

'I hope you've brought me something personal from Emily?'

'I think she burned the midnight oil finishing the last one for you.'

'Bless her. I am very lucky with my relations,' Bea said airily.

'Whose relations? You merit lace cloths and doilies but she hasn't made you a whole bedspread,' Emma said smugly. 'And I've known her for longer.'

'I shall telephone her late tonight to thank her. You may have a word too if you are good and haven't drunk too much wine.'

'What had you in mind?'

'Dwight really dropped me in this one, and you and I share everything don't we, Ducky?'

'I think this is the night I wash my hair.'

'C'mon! You've done it before in England. Remember the Italian officers we met at the General's house in Epsom?' Bea's laugh was malicious and very amused.

'Oh, *no*! Not again. I was pinched at least five times and I couldn't avoid noticing that one was getting very excited when we danced.'

'You were much too young and in-experienced to know that such things came up during a purely social occasion,' Bea spluttered, then looked dreamy. 'Did you know that Dwight wore a cricket box when he was pursuing me so that he could control his pants and appear normal? Poor lamb. I couldn't think what was in there and it wasn't something that one asked while Joe Loss was playing a rumba or one of the big bands was playing something very cheek to cheek.'

'I had forgotten what a bad influence you are. Tell me what the evening will bring. At least we have stalwart husbands now to protect us.'

'This is a mixed diplomatic bag; some French, some Scandinavian and a few Americans and Canadians. They all speak English but I do make an effort to talk to the French in their own language as they are a bit touchy that French is no longer the main diplomatic language worldwide. Pa taught me that one, and I have been given some very nice French perfume on occasion as a result of my tactfulness,' Bea said complacently. 'Cocktail dresses and welcoming smiles, but not too welcoming as my husband will begin to mutter and threaten an international incident.' She sighed, theatrically. 'The demented creature thinks I am still the lovely girl he married.'

'You know damn well you are and he adores you.'

'Nice, isn't it?' Bea seized her arm. 'We can have fun being beautiful but correct. They find it a 'real turn on' as they say over here. We must count the times we are called, 'jus wunnerful' and 'formidable'. I don't know what the Scandinavians say, but it will be fun finding out if they are as dour as they look.'

Twelve

'My, my, you surely are a couple of hand-some beaux. I sure will enjoy being danced by you'all,' Bea said with a heavy Southern drawl.

'Less of the Scarlett O'Hara,' Dwight said but his face was aglow with approval and affection. His white tuxedo was immaculate and the row of decorations in miniature showed just what he had done in the American Air Force and how important he was now in diplomatic circles.

Emma smiled at Paul and her eyes sparkled. Bea wasn't the only one to have such a good-looking husband. Paul's well-cut but more sober black dinner-jacket and neatly tied bow-tie contrasted with the pleated white shirt, and the lean cut of his trousers showed the firm but graceful lines of his thighs. His eyes showed the golden flecks that indicated that he was happy and relaxed and Emma knew that he needed this break from patients and their worries and the strain of being responsible for the well-being of sick minds.

'No dancing yet and you will have to join the line up,' Bea said. 'I shall be very picky tonight.'

'Right! First you smile but not too much and be nice to the ambassadors but not too nice. I'm fresh out of duelling pistols,' Dwight said dryly.

Bea giggled. 'Steer me in the direction of the Scandinavians. They might be less volatile than the French. Bad luck, Ducky. You take the Latins and the French and one lecherous husband of a very good friend who deserves better. The blood won't muss up Paul's nice dark jacket if it comes to blows.'

'Behave!' Emma whispered as they came closer to the row of distinguished guests.

The introductions over, the guests mingled and Bea introduced Emma to some people she knew well, including the lecherous husband of her good friend. 'You can't keep her to yourselves,' Dwight warned.

'She is on duty tonight and I expect her to charm Monsieur Martine.'

'That's real mean,' Jepherson Pyke said and held Emma's hand firmly for a full minute. Emma let her hand stay limply in his, having found from experience that if she seemed to have no reaction to his touch, the man would soon release her, embarrassed by his lack of success.

Bea grinned, knowing exactly what was happening. 'I see that you remember Heath Cross dances,' she said, and Jepherson looked puzzled.

'Hospital dances, but not ones as glamorous as this evening,' Emma said hastily. 'This is fun,' she added now that at least a few feet separated them.

Paul raised an eyebrow and came to her side. 'Sorry to drag you away, Darling, but the group over there are waiting to meet you, Dwight told me.'

Bea had deserted her and was deep in conversation with an elderly Frenchman who, having kissed both her hands, now stood and looked at her as if she was a piece of delicious meringue that he wanted to eat but had no means of doing so.

'You look far too pretty for this crowd,' Paul whispered. 'Shall we run away together?'

'Too tempting but I have work to do,' Emma replied sternly. 'Besides I'm enjoying myself. Go and chat up a few American matrons. They'll love it.'

'Just watch that dimple. It's showing, and isn't good for local morale. There will be others apart from me who want to kiss it.'

'Stop flirting with your wife and let Emma come with me,' Dwight growled. 'I'll find you someone who I think needs a psychiatrist! I didn't ask you over here to slack off and hog one of the only two pretty women here.' He held Emma's arm in a proprietorial way. 'Get lost, Paul. Emma's dress goes better with my tuxedo than it does with your mortician's black.'

'Now what?' asked Emma.

'You wanted to meet the Swedes and I'll feel safer if you and Bea stick with them this evening. They are solemn and take life seriously. My wife needs a slap on the butt when she looks at men in a certain way.'

'She likes to be friendly,' Emma asserted. 'And she is only doing her duty by being charming to her husband's diplomatic contacts. Both of us are here to please, Sir! We are willing to work really hard for you.' Her lips twitched. 'You know it means nothing.'

'I know it, you know it and Bea knows it but the poor guys who see her smiling at them don't know it.'

'She can handle men,' Emma said briskly. 'You didn't see her with thirty healthy earthy types with nothing wrong with them except for broken limbs which did nothing to dull their libido!'

Dwight grinned. 'I can imagine. C'mon and meet some real people. This only needs my godfather here to make this one of the parties we had at Epsom.'

'It's better.' Emma spoke softly. 'I have Paul now.'

He glanced at her and nodded, his expression gentle. 'He's good for you, Emma.'

'I'm starving.' Bea stood near the huge buffet decorated with exotic flower arrangements and spotless damask table coverings.

Delicate porcelain and colourful linen napkins grouped round champagne flutes and wine glasses where people were helping themselves to lobster, prime beef and lamb and various intricate dishes and salads. Bea's Frenchman handed her a glass of champagne and an empty plate. 'Thank you,' she said and put the glass down on a table. 'I'll choose some food first as I can't handle a glass at the same time.'

Dwight casually changed the champagne for a glass of white wine and gave Emma the same. 'Can't have you two getting the blues,' he whispered. 'Bea is fine most of the time but with you here she might go down memory lane and find it strewn with weeds.'

'You are an angel,' Emma replied and knew that he recalled the time when champagne reminded them both of the death of a dear friend in the Blitz which made it the one wine that for years they had been unable to drink with any enjoyment.

The Air Force dance band played softly in the background and when the guests moved away from the food into the parquet-floored arena, changed tempo and played the latest dance tunes. Saxophones brought haunting memories but these were good memories and the dancing couples made a rainbow of colour as they moved across the wide room. Emma saw her reflection in the long mirrors on the panelled walls, and the bright expensive clothes of the other guests, and was glad that she had spent far more than she had ever done on clothes for this visit.

'You dance very well,' said Hans, the fair-haired Swedish diplomat who Dwight had brought to meet her, thinking that he was harmless but possibly boring. Dwight was conscious of the fact that Emma and Bea were making a very definite impression on men who were vulnerable to the charms of fresh British complexions and bright interested eyes.

During a pause in the dancing, Bea whispered, 'Aunt Maggie, alias my dear husband, is the perfect chaperon. He steered me away from an absolutely divine Spaniard who looks like a matador and has the most heavenly wicked mouth.'

'Remember you are a godly and sober matron with three children,' Emma retorted. 'What happened to that demure expression you promised to wear tonight?'

'We dance again,' Hans said when the music started once more, and Bea looked amused, then mildly puzzled, seeing the solemn Nordic face.

'I like this tune,' Emma said. 'I once had the record and we wore it out at hospital dances, using it until it was too scratched to play.'

'I, too, remember it.'

'Where did you hear it?'

'In hospital, in England. When we were convalescing, we were invited to what they called the 'hops' and they played this tune very often, but this is the first time I have danced to it.'

'And did you have to listen to "An Apple for the Teacher?"'

Hans looked animated. 'And "Who's taking you home tonight?" when there was nobody for us to take home,' he said eagerly.

Emma experienced a sharp vision of déjà vu and saw an emaciated pale-faced man with unkempt blond hair and dark shadows under his eyes, sitting apart, away from the rough splintery dance floor of the recreation room at Heath Cross, the military sector hospital attached to Beatties. Elbow crutches rested against a chair and by special request, Edith Piaf's throaty French voice came over the slowly dancing crowd of nurses, students and doctors with a sprinkling of nearly healed patients, passionately asserting that she regretted nothing. At the time there had much to regret and Emma had been lonely, too.

'Where was this?' she asked but she already knew. 'Were you in Nurse Shuter's ward?'

Hans stumbled and lost his achieved American nonchalance, with a very American and un-Nordic expletive. 'I thought it could not be her.' He stared at Bea who was laughing up into the face of her Frenchman. 'Nurse Shuter is Mrs Miller?'

'We all looked different then, in uniform after hectic days of anxiety and hard work,' Emma said gently. 'I do remember you with elbow crutches and a plaster cast on one wrist. There was no doubt that you were a patient as you wore hospital blue to mark you as an ambulant service patient who had recovered sufficiently to be allowed out on buses and into the local town and pubs. As I recall the locals were generous and let you travel free most of the time and gave you good service in cafés.'

'Why did you remember me?' His eyes gleamed with pleasure. 'Why me when there were so many there?'

'There were only five patients there that night and Bea was in charge of seeing that they had their fair share of the curled-up sandwiches and cider before the ravenous students hogged it all. I helped and kept an eye on your group as I thought that two of you might faint with all the excitement of one of our dances,' she added dryly.

He laughed and he lost the air of polite formality. 'I thought that life was bad, but looking back it was good, a little more than I knew.'

'And now you are completely better?'

'Most of the time, when I am back in my own country.'

'And at other times, when you are in

America and England?'

'I mourn for the destruction of beautiful buildings in London and here I mourn because many people have not seen what others have seen and suffered.'

'The war is over, Korea is over, and you are an important man,' Emma said gently. 'All this is on the surface and hides a lot of feelings.'

'I know that now. Were you here for Memorial Day on May the thirtieth?'

She shook her head. 'I have a lot to learn about America. I know about Thanksgiving and how that originated when the first immigrants had a safe landing and gave thanks, but what is Memorial Day?'

'I was out there on the plaza by the White House this year and the edges of the sky were purple as they had been the day I was wounded in France. There were thousands of people, listening to speeches and hearing patriotic tunes and many men were crying. They commemorate all the wars from the War of Independence to the present day and have much memory of recent wars when their own people were killed. I realised that under some of the less pleasant aspects of this country, there is real feeling and memories of sorrow. It was good for me. I come from a less spontaneous people, but on that day I wept, too.' He laughed uneasily. 'I am boring you.'

'No.' Emma blinked to hide her own emotion. 'I would have joined you.'

The last triumphant chords of 'Yes Sir, that's my baby' crashed to a noisy conclusion and they walked across to Bea and her partner. Bea held out a hand and smiled at Hans. 'Complicated fracture of tib and fib and a Colles' fracture of one wrist, plus shrapnel in the chest,' she said briskly. 'I knew I'd seen you somewhere.'

The Frenchman looked very confused. *'Comment?'*

Bea gave him a ravishing smile. 'Dance with Mrs Sykes, monsieur. I have met an old friend.'

'This tib and fib is a joke?'

'Not exactly; an old war wound, but it's better now. Hans promised to dance with me when he was better and he never did, so now I demand my rights.'

'*Formidable*,' the Frenchman said, looking after Bea. He held Emma lightly and she found that he danced well, and the lack of communication between them due to her not speaking much French was hardly noticeable.

Dwight and Paul did their duty, dancing with wives of the various diplomats and as Bea remarked, totting up points for America. 'And Britain,' Emma insisted.

'Who told them I was a psychiatrist?' Paul asked when at last he sank onto a chaise longue in a glassed-in annexe with Bea, who had seen that he was being pursued by a determined lady of vast proportions and had rescued him. 'You are a genius, Bea. She was impressed when you told her that I was wanted on the phone and I hope I never shall discover why she hated her father and wet the bed until she was nine.'

Bea giggled. 'I didn't exactly say that the President needed you but I did murmur 'White House'. I'm afraid the staff here are far too meticulous. One of the aides made a list of guests and their occupations and you were billed on it. Cheer up. We can go home soon. Dwight looks exhausted after trying to speak and understand Spanish. Maybe now he'll take a few lessons. He's put it off for long enough and the Hispanic influence is growing all the time.'

'I've been amazed at the many different faces and cultures here. America really is a melting pot of every nationality,' Paul declared.

Bea looked sad. 'The original promises have been watered down a little. All those hopeful immigrants coming here under the shadow of the Statue of Liberty must have had high hopes of a wonderful future and a good living, but so many faced poverty and disappointment.' She shrugged. 'I don't know the answer but I do see a lot of suffering when I go into the big cities.'

'I haven't seen many signs of depression among the crowds in the shops. Maybe they are philosophical about their lives.'

Bea smiled slightly. 'One good thing is that they have a more optimistic view of poverty here. It is not a sin to be poor and they believe that every American regardless of race and penury could have the opportunity to be President if the cookie crumbled their way. Personal merit and hard work is valued over wealthy parents and family history. The son of a tramp is respected if he pulls himself up by his bootlaces and becomes a captain of industry. Such progress is a cause for pride. They see no need to hang fake portraits of "ancestors" on their walls to prove how highly born they are.'

'It's what you have done personally, not who your ancestors were that counts,' Paul agreed.

Yellow taxis and private vehicles took away the guests and Dwight and his party went home in an official limousine.

'You can stay with us as long as you like,' Dwight said. 'You were a real hit tonight and I had to fend off a string of invitations that I don't think you'd enjoy.'

'Including I hope, the lady with the purple feather boa and enormous caftan?' Paul asked hopefully.

Bea laughed. 'I thought that she would engulf you under that caftan and carry you off to give her a *very* intimate consultation.'

'She hinted that she needed at least six

consultations to sort out her wounded libido,' Paul said wryly. 'Next time I go to one of your parties, Dwight, I shall wear dark glasses and a heavy black beard.'

'They'd love it, and take you for Dr Freud.' Dwight grinned, but Paul knew he was serious when he said, 'You should come here for keeps, Paul. You are just what this mentally unstable country needs and you could make a fortune in private practice. Analysis is a very fashionable must for film stars and important people, as a necessary addition to life, and we need good men like you to drive away the charlatans.'

Paul shook his head. 'We have enough inadequates at home to keep me busy for years and we like London, and of course we need Aunt Emily and the Isle of Wight.

'Don't,' Bea said pathetically, 'You make me homesick for her apple pies and lovely bread.' She glanced cautiously at her husband. 'If Dwight gets a posting to Whitehall you might see more of us than you want.'

'Is that likely?'

'Not for years,' Dwight said firmly. 'I just

keep the idea in her head so that she thinks we are nearly there, but there's a lot to do first.' He led Paul away to look at a modern painting and asked what he thought of it and Emma was left with Bea for a while.

'Would you really come back for a while? What about the children's education?'

'We talk about that but can't decide what we want. My father would like the boys to go to his old school and a British university but I am not so keen. I've seen some of the dimwits and crooks they turn out in the dear old school.'

'Your father is a successful businessman and a Member of Parliament,' Emma pointed out. 'He also has great charm and a famous wife, so the school can't be all bad.'

Bea screwed up her handkerchief and frowned. 'He wasn't like that at one time. He sowed enough wild oats to supply a porridge factory and do you remember my cousin, dear Major Ripley who had charm, a marvellous war record and a snake-like fascination for little rabbits, and tried to rape you? He went to the dear old school too.'

'If Dwight was posted to England, you'd have to decide on somewhere.'

'Not for ages yet,' Bea said comfortably. 'All I want for the babes is a peaceful, safe and happy childhood, with visits to you sometimes, and then the miracle of the perfect school wherever it might be, here or on the other side of the drink.'

'Does Dwight want them to board? George is sending Clive away as he will need a certain continuity if his parents move around in the Navy.' Emma laughed. 'At least that's what George thinks but, of course, Emily has other ideas – Margaret his new wife will have a baby as soon as possible after they are married and stay in Hampshire until the baby is old enough to travel around, and if Clive isn't to feel unwanted and shunted off to school when the new baby is born, I can see little Clive attending the local day school for a while.'

'What does Emily see for my infants?'

'Nothing bad,' Emma said hastily and tried to forget that her aunt had suggested that little Mark might need care.

As if sensing what was in Emma's mind,

Bea gave her a hard look. 'I worry about Mark at times. He's so tiny but as Emily would say, he's a wilful child and difficult to keep in one place, like a ball of mercury. I'm glad you brought a set of reins for him, and he wanted to wear them as soon as he saw Rose wearing hers. He pretends to be a horse but they just might keep him from running off when we are in a big store.'

Dwight kissed the back of her neck. 'Bed and a busy day tomorrow, Honey. I'm all tied up with official business here but I've told Chris that he must be ready to drive you wherever you want to go and suggested he make a tour of the Capitol. Why not leave the children with Nanny for the morning and see the sights in peace?'

'Count me out too,' Paul said apologetically. 'I have to see the Harvard people and plan the tour, so I shall have to catch up with you later for dinner.'

'Just you and me, Emma. What fun! Nobody to tell us not to linger in the dress shops.'

'This is a cultural tour,' Dwight admonished.

'We need to know what's being worn by the great and the good,' Bea replied sweetly. 'We can have lunch and go to an exhibition that I've wanted to see but I knew would bore Dwight as it's very modern art.'

Thirteen

'Just drop us off by the park and I'll call you when we are finished with shopping, Chris. That will be about four. In fact let's make it four p.m. outside the plaza gates and we can be home to play with the children for an hour after they have tea.'

'Yes, Ma'am,' Chris replied and asked if there were any errands he could do on the way back to the house.

'Go home first, then collect the bundle of clothes for dry-cleaning and take it along, and take this message for the stables. There will be a waterproof jacket for Mark to bring back from the saddlery shop, but you can leave it in the car as he will want it when we go down to the river. That's all. You are free until you pick us up later.'

'This is like old times,' Emma said with satisfaction. 'Our precious day off from Beatties was something to fill with anything more exciting than work and today feels like that. We can do as we please!'

They strolled along the wide road edged with well-tended trees fronting smart dress shops, and saw so many wonderful creations that it was impossible to choose which was more attractive than the others and would be perfect for them.

'I want something smart and practical,' Bea said firmly. 'I don't think we'll find it here. These are marvellous and completely impossible, and designed by someone who has never had a child within a hundred yards of her or him, and very expensive.' She sighed. 'Just as well to move on. Dwight would have a fit if I bought that one,' Bea told her, pointing to a gauzy creation that might look good on a skinny model on a catwalk but would not stand up to sticky fingers and pony hair. 'The sacrifices I make for my children,' she laughed.

'And worth every bit,' Emma said. 'I can't think how I existed before we had Rose, but I know how couples without children must think we are a bit biased and far too absorbed by our own tots.'

'It's good that you have joined the club and understand about colic at three in the morning and tantrums when bedtime is imminent; at least we have them with Mark at times, but Rose is so good I don't believe it's true.'

'Next time have a girl,' Emma suggested.

'You're the one who should be having morning sickness. One little girl is nothing,' Bea told her.

'I'm thinking about it,' Emma confessed.

'Ask Emily.'

'No! She might make me feel guilty.'

Lunch in a salad bar was good and the food imaginative. 'Reminds me of the Quality Inn where we ate in Leicester Square during the war. That was the first American place we found and the food was always good, if a trifle odd at times. I'm still not sure if I like goat, but we ate it as it was off-ration.' Emma looked thoughtful. 'It was where your cousin Eddy Ripley appeared and you tried to brush him off.'

'My completely evil but nationally heroic cousin. Do you still have his cap badge?'

'Somewhere tucked away in a drawer. I

couldn't throw it away, could I?'

'No, Ducky. He was a part of your education and a grim warning about men, but I'm glad he died.' Emma looked shocked. 'Not just because of what he tried to do to you, Emma. If he had lived he would have ruined a lot of girls and become a real menace to society, once the war was over. Cheer up! I don't have any more awful cousins and my father is now a pillar of propriety and besotted with Miranda, so he's no threat to young virgins.'

'He is coming over to see Miranda's first night in New York, isn't he?'

'Soon, and he'll visit us here with her for a weekend when the play has settled down and she can leave the cast for a night or two.'

'Is it time to get back?' Emma asked.

'There's a café by the plaza where Chris will know where to find us, so we'll wait there. I need to sit down. We've walked for miles and these shoes are killing me.'

After a second cup of coffee, Bea glanced at her watch for the third time and Emma saw that it was twenty past four.

'Not like him to be late,' Bea said, and

looked worried.

'Maybe we should wait outside,' Emma suggested.

'Yes.' Bea stood up and walked out into the sunshine. She waved to a car that was driving slowly along the edge of the walkway and the driver stopped when she saw Bea. 'What's wrong?' By now Bea was running towards the car and Emma followed closely, Bea's apprehension making them move urgently. 'Jan? Where's Chris and the limo?"

The children's nanny looked pale. 'Chris told me to collect you. I can't manage the limo, so I drove this smaller car.'

'Why?' Bea's voice was low and yet seemed to be under a desperate control. 'It's one of the boys, isn't it?'

'Mark is missing.' The girl burst into tears and Emma saw that she was in no fit state to drive.

'Move over,' she said briskly. 'I'd better drive.'

Bea nodded wordlessly and climbed in beside her, leaving the now incoherent girl to sit in the back seat.

The road signs were clear and Emma

gritted her teeth and drove carefully, trying not to think of a possible accident as she had never driven an American car before now, or on the right-hand side of the road.

'Where is Chris?' Bea asked. 'Snap out of it girl, I need to know.'

'He's looking for Mark. We saw him this morning and then Karen, the nursery nurse, said he didn't come in to lunch.'

'She was supposed to be with them all the time,' Bea said bleakly. Emma recalled the overweight and rather offhand girl who Bea suspected didn't do her duty very well, but as she was amiable and liked by the children she was kept on the staff to double up for the real nanny when she needed a break or was absorbed by the twins.

'Did Mark play her up this morning?'

'He ran down to the gates three times and hid behind a tree to scare her and she brought him back each time then told him to stay indoors until she fetched him for lunch. She was grumbling that he was being tiresome and had worn her out.'

'Where did she go?'

'She helped Chris put the clothes in the

car for the dry-cleaners and then I think she sat on the swing couch under the awning until it was lunchtime. I saw Chris return from the stables and put the car in the driveway, after he'd taken some gear out of the trunk of the limo and he'd gone to close the main gates.'

'He left the gates open?'

'Only for a minute or so,' Jan said quickly. 'The gardener was nowhere to be seen when Chris drove through and sounded the horn. It's his job to close the gates, but when Chris noticed that he didn't arrive he hurried back to close the gates himself.'

'It takes less than a minute,' Bea said worriedly, 'Mark is like an eel. He could be anywhere.'

'Karen is very upset,' Jan ventured.

'So she should be! If anything happens to Mark I shall turn her over to the police and say she is responsible.' The passion and grief in her voice was terrifying.

Emma parked behind the big car that Chris had as yet left in the driveway, as he'd expected to use it to pick up his employer and her friend.

'Where are the other children?' Emma had a lump in her throat. She was desperately worried about Mark too, but a guilty tinge of relief persisted that Rose wasn't involved.

'Rose is having a nap and the twins are playing in the walled garden.'

Bea frowned. 'Mark has his nap now and if he doesn't sleep for an hour he is impossible and naughty. If he has wandered out through the gateway and been picked up by someone he could be at risk, as he might be very difficult.' She hid her eyes for a moment then braced herself and said firmly, 'What's been done? Have you alerted the police and tried to contact my husband?'

'Chris is out on his motorcycle, touring the streets and park and one police car is already here and there is another coming up the drive. Mr Miller has been contacted and should be on his way.'

The police officer was brisk and wasted no time on pleasantries. His business-like manner had a calming influence and Bea was glad to let him take some of the strain. 'Who had care of the child and where was

270

she when he was missed?'

Jan told him the bare facts.

'I want to see her *now*. How long has she been employed here and has she been efficient in the past? Any boyfriends, any relatives calling here? Anything like suspicious characters in the grounds? Any spooky phonecalls for anyone?'

Karen was still in tears and the officer viewed her with ill-concealed contempt. 'Cool it, Lady. I need to know what happened. What is your part in all this?' He regarded her with great distrust and she sobbed and couldn't speak so he turned away muttering, 'Fat, useless broad.'

Two of his men waited for instructions.

'You don't know if he left the estate so let's start right here. You go down to the gates and ask anyone including the bums by the wall over there if they've seen the boy.' Jan handed over a picture of the child to one of the policemen. 'You search the house,' the officer ordered the other man, and told Jan to go with him. He half smiled at Bea. 'You'd be surprised, Ma'am, how many times we find missing persons inside. I had a dog once, scared of thunder, who went missing and after we searched the woods we found him hiding under a bed.'

'We'll look in the outhouses,' Bea said, obviously relieved to have something to do.

'Maybe the gardener knows something. You said he was on gate duty?'

The boy who helped in the vegetable garden shook his head. 'He had to go to bed a while ago as he had the gripes. Something he ate, he said.'

'Where is he? I want to speak to him. Maybe he has the gripes maybe not.' The officer's voice was grim. 'Take me to his quarters and I'll judge for myself how bad he is.'

A distant droning became louder and they looked up at the helicopter circling the house. 'They got in touch with Dwight,' Bea said with relief. 'I thought he might be at the old airport and he got my message.'

A flurry of dusty air made them turn away until the rotors stopped and Dwight flung open the door and hurried over from the helipad. He saw the tense faces and knew that no progress had been made. Bea rushed into his arms and he held her tightly, his face drawn and anxious.

Bea pushed him away gently. 'I'm okay. We were about to search the outbuildings. You take the path behind the swimming pool and we'll go that way.'

'The pool?'

'Not there. They looked there first. The men are looking over the house and asking passers-by, and the last ones to come are going to join Chris in the streets.'

'Let's go.' Dwight touched her cheek and smiled. 'That's my girl. Chin up,' he said and sprinted along the path to the patch of woodland behind the pool.

An eerie silence was broken only by the sounds of feet trampling the long grass behind the pool and the clunk of doors opening and shutting as the outhouses were searched. Bea sent Jan to telephone Eve at the stables in case Mark had wandered that way. He knew where to go and was fascinated by horses, but Jan shook her head and said that Eve had seen nothing but would watch the road in case she saw him.

Karen seemed in a kind of torpor unable

to move and unable to speak coherently and everyone ignored her.

The searchers gathered by the front entrance for further instructions as no trace of Mark had been found except for one small scuffed sandal that Bea found behind the limo. She held it tightly as if to absorb his vibrations and prayed that Aunt Emily had been right and that nothing terrible would happen to any of her children.

Emma recalled that her aunt had remarked that Mark needed watching but had given no hint from her fey mind that any dark cloud hung over him.

'What now?' Bea sounded fraught. 'Mark has eaten no lunch and must be hungry and very tired. I should have been far more strict and made sure he never speaks to strangers, but he likes people and I couldn't make him suspicious of everyone who comes here.'

Emma went into the house to see if Rose was awake and hoped that she had not been frightened by uniformed policemen with guns in hip holsters, looking in her room.

Rose held out her arms and her face was pink with sleep. 'I want to play now,' she said. 'I want Mark.'

Emma hugged her, revelling in the softness and sweet smell of flower-scented talc and she kissed the dimpled cheek, so like her own and promising the same beauty. 'Not now, Darling. Mark is ... isn't here just now.'

Rose chuckled. 'He's hiding.' She struggled out of bed and handed Emma her sandals. 'Help me, Mummy. I want to find Mark.'

Emma buckled the leather sandals and thought of the one that Bea now held so tightly as a kind of talisman.

As soon as she was dressed, Rose ran from the room and avoided Emma's restraining hands. She blinked in the bright sunlight and regarded the group of solemn grown-ups with reservation, her normal shyness asserting itself, then she sidled over to the limo and stood by the tailgate of the trunk.

'When did you see Mark?' Emma asked.

'Not telling. He's hiding.' Rose giggled and pushed a fist into her mouth.

'He didn't have lunch. Did you see him after lunch?'

Rose shook her head vigorously. She liked this game.

'Before lunch, out here?' Emma forced herself to be calm but wanted to shake her darling daughter and she could see that Bea had the same urge. Inspired, as she had a feeling that Rose knew more than anyone there, Emma said with a lightness that she didn't feel, 'Count up to three and call him and then go and find him. Show us where he's hiding.'

'Close eyes first?' Rose suggested. 'Everyone close eyes?'

Later, Bea dissolved into tears of a kind of irritated joy as she described how three tough policemen and a sprinkling of staff put their hands over their eyes on the orders of a three-year-old.

'Mark!' Rose bellowed and tapped on the door of the car trunk. Bea ran and opened the stiff door and almost crumpled up on the rough tarmac, then stood and reached into the large space and picked up a sleepy and rather cantankerous boy.

'I'm hungry,' he said, fighting off Bea's tight hugs. 'Someone shut the lid and I fell asleep but I've had my nap and I want some fried bacon.'

Dwight came running and Emma could have wept to see the relief on his face, but he said gruffly, 'Boys who hide and worry people do not have bacon and pancakes. They have bread and cheese and milk.' Mark turned away from him and ran into the house to find the cook and Dwight grinned weakly. 'Do we beat him or love him?' he asked. 'Just now I want to do both.' Bea clung to him and their relief was full of tearful laughter. Chris appeared with a tray of bagels and sandwiches for the policemen and Dwight went in to fetch Coke and root beer and fresh orange juice.

'Nobody was really to blame,' Emma said. 'Don't be too hard on Karen. I think she has had a very bad shock and you may find that she is almost too careful in future if you give her another chance.'

'I'll think about it.' Bea sounded grim and Emma wondered if Karen would ever be trusted again. Jan fetched the twins from the small garden and they took Rose with them to find strawberries in the kitchen gardens.

'If you sack Karen, you still need a nursery nurse,' Emma pointed out. 'It means getting used to a fresh face and another unknown person to care for the children. At least you know the worst of Karen now. She's honest and she is very upset.'

'I need some coffee,' Bea said. 'I feel as if I've been kicked by a mule.' Chris brought a tray out to the terrace and Dwight hastily drank a cup of coffee and took a large bite from a bagel. 'Gotta go,' he said and ran towards the waiting helicopter. 'Maybe they will still be chewing the fat over minor details and I'll not have missed anything.'

Emma poured coffee and looked at Bea's pale face. 'What a lot can happen in an hour.'

'What a lot could have happened in five minutes if ... if–' Bea burst into tears.

Fourteen

'I envy you Boston.' Bea looked sad.

'I'd rather stay here.' Emma glanced out at the wide garden. The scent of freshly cut grass filled the air as the gardener swept past the terrace on the sit-on mower and the air stirred.

'It's going to be warm and that means that Mark will be fractious if last year is any guide. Washington in summer is humid and hot and even though we are above the city, we still feel it.'

'It's only pleasantly warm as yet,' protested Emma. She glanced at Bea's set face and shook her head. 'Come on now, we shall only be away for a few weeks and then we all go to the mountains. Your father and Miranda will visit you while we are away and it's time that you realised that Mark and the twins are safe.'

'I know, but that scare really threw me

even though nothing happened. I saw the expression on that officer's face when he spoke to Karen. He had her labelled child molester or worse and I knew that he must deal with dozens of cases where children are hurt or killed. Sometimes I hate America and everything in it.'

'No you don't!' Emma spoke sharply. 'It's because you are so happy here that you reacted as you did when something threatened to spoil it for you. You love it here; you have Dwight and the children and a good life, Bea, and Dwight is far too busy to need you throwing a wobbly.'

'Yes, Sister Dewar.' A slight smile began to spread into a chuckle. 'You are right of course. When were you ever wrong, but I hate to see you go away. See what a spoiled bitch I have become. I might have known I'd get no sympathy from you. I hear Jan calling the twins, so we'd best go down to the car and hopefully wear them out on the horses before they go to bed.' Bea glanced at her watch. 'Dwight said he'd be home early and wants us here, so we have only an hour or so to spare.'

Eve quickly allocated the ponies to the children and two stable girls took Rose and Mark on leading reins round the exercise yard and into the paddock while Emma and Bea sat in the shade and drank freshly squeezed orange juice from tall glasses filled with ice.

'I admit that America has *some* advantages,' Bea said, topping up her glass with more juice. 'When did you ever have unlimited juice back home?'

'One orange is a treat at home,' Emma agreed. 'And the rest?'

'Good coffee, wonderful steaks and corn meal muffins, lobsters flown in from Maine and friendly people,' Bea allowed. 'Just one thing missing ... the Sykes are not here forever.'

'The Atlantic has shrunk since you came over, Bea. I shall never think of you as far away again. Admit it, you feel the same and we both know that at any time we can cross over and never feel isolated.'

'If we decide to have the children educated in England, it will make a wonderful excuse for me to visit you several times a year.' Bea looked better, without the tightening of her mouth that showed she still suffered from the effects of Mark's escapade. 'The trouble with me,' she said slowly, 'is that I had such a lousy family and a lot of emotional neglect that I want everything now and can't get enough of friendship – real friendship – and love, and I shall make sure that the children have it all.'

'They do have it all,' Emma replied softly. 'It shows, Bea, but don't overdo the material things. They don't need that.'

'I suppose you are about to tell me how you had nothing but a bouncy ball and a set of playing cards when you were little and were blissfully happy,' Bea reported tartly.

'I wasn't blissfully happy and I wasn't allowed cards. My mother said they were the work of the devil,' Emma said mildly. 'You and I have a lot to forget about our families, and now is the time to enjoy life.'

Bea looked almost accusing. 'You have Aunt Emily and Janey and your precious island with all those noisy seagulls and damp grass!'

'And we both had Beatties and Heath Cross and so much fun in between the hard work and sadness. We probably had more experience of real emotion than most people have in a lifetime.'

'I know. Take no notice of me; I see it all the time and know that I am really, really lucky. Some people have such empty lives. It's just that ... since we nearly lost Mark, or thought we had, I wonder about the future.' She cast her eyes up and her hands supplicated in a mock dramatic gesture. 'Aunt Emily where are you when I need you?'

'Eve is waving; time to collect the children and get back. Dwight wants us there as he has something for us, or so he hinted.'

'Mummy, look at me,' Johnny called. He had a scarf round his neck and a battered hat over one eye. 'I'm Roy Rogers and this is my horse Trigger. I want a real Wild West hat and spurs.'

'Ask Daddy when we get to Texas,' Bea suggested. She helped her son down from the saddle and hugged him. 'Time to go, Cowboy.'

'I *do* want a real hat.'

'First, you must ride a lot better and be more like Roy Rogers,' Bea teased him. She whispered. 'We are all going to the cinema tomorrow to see Trigger, but don't tell Mark yet.'

'Are you going to buy him the clothes?' Emma asked.

'Certainly not!' Bea laughed. 'I've already told my father that if he buys a few Wild West duds for the two boys he will be their friend for life. Funny! Pa never bought me the right presents but he has changed a lot over the years. Miranda has a lot to do with that and I have shown him the folly of his misspent youth.'

'You have?' Emma's disbelief was comical.

'I told him that if I hadn't gone to Beatties and met some soul mates who had a few morals, I would have been as bad as he and my mother were, sleeping around and never really knowing love.' She chuckled. 'He looked shattered and said he had no idea that I'd ever known what he did, swore he'd always cared for me and been proud of me and actually asked me to forgive him.'

'And now he is the perfect father, grand-father and devoted husband.'

'Come on, we can't wait all day,' Dwight called as he opened the car door.

'Yes, *Sir*. See, Emma, I attract bullies. What is it now? An inarticulate corn-bred senator to smile at and give him English tea?'

Dwight glanced at his watch and hurried them into the house, leaving Jan to take the children. 'Hector assured me the time would be right and being the perfect public relations officer he's usually right. Because of the congress, the overseas calls have had to be stacked all this week, but there he is and as far as that man can smile, he's smiling. I tried to reach Emily a few times but even she has to sleep. She should be drinking that god-awful tea by now and stirring the fire ready for the day.' He took the receiver from Hector. 'Hi there, beau-tiful.'

'Let me,' Bea begged and he laughed, said a few more words and handed the phone over to the two women. 'I suppose you'll pull rank, Dewar. Be quick, I want to speak to her.'

'What a nice surprise. I can hear you as clearly as if you were in this room.'

'It's almost as good as that. How are you – and Aunt Janey?'

'Is everything all right with you and those youngsters? I had a bad head a few days ago and I couldn't shake off a feeling but it went all of a sudden and I think they are fine now?'

'Nothing bad happened but Mark hid and gave us all a scare,' Emma said. 'We can't have long on the line and Bea wants to talk to you.'

'Good. I think she's worried so I'll say goodbye to you and give my love to the children and Paul.'

'Aunt Emily?' Bea sounded like a child asking an adult for a favour and Emma saw how much her contact with Emily meant to her.

'I hear that Mark is giving you trouble. Don't lose any sleep over that rapscallion. My mother would have said he was like my brother Jack, as slippery as an eel, in and out of trouble and never a scratch on him.'

'It made me edgy,' Bea admitted.

'And so it should. Being as you are, in a foreign country with all that crime, you need to be careful, but I see no real harm for you and yours. One thing that may be not important, but came to me. Have you a man who does work for you? Younger than middle-aged and a good worker, who works outside, but I am sure he comes into the house when you are out?' There was a pause and Bea knew that Emily was being fey.

'We have an undergardener who's been with us for six months and we like him.'

'That's as may be. Be careful of your nice things. He's a bit light-fingered. Did you have references?'

'I'm not sure. I think he's a relation of the gardener, so he might have vouched for him. I'll get the office to check him out.'

'Just as well to be careful. You need to be a bit more careful locking up drawers, my girl. What's that noise?'

'That's to say we must ring off. Bless you, dear Aunt Emily. I can afford to lose a brooch or two, but not my children.'

'Everything okay?' asked Emma. 'Next

287

time I'd like to talk to her,' she added dryly.

'You are safe and healthy. It's my mind that needed sorting out.'

'And did she do that?'

'Of course.'

'But there was something?'

'Do you remember me asking if you'd seen that turquoise scarf pin I wore last week?'

'You left it on your dressing table after you changed for that cocktail party and we were in a hurry to leave.'

'I said I'd lock it away later,' Bea said bleakly, 'but I forgot and now I have no idea where it is.'

'Have you asked the cleaner?'

'She looked everywhere and said I must have put it away somewhere safe, and I let it ride as she hates anything that might accuse her of stealing.'

'Has the oracle spoken?' asked Dwight.

'She suggested that we beat our children every day and give Mark to a home for bad boys.'

'Liar! What did she say?' Dwight eyed his wife and grinned. 'She told you that all is well with the Miller family and that you can rest easy.'

'My, you are as bad as Emily!' Bea kissed his cheek. 'Thanks Pal, I needed to hear her voice.'

'So I can eat dinner and not have to wonder if you are okay?'

'There was one thing.'

He sighed. 'If the kids are fine, I can take it. Tell me the worst.'

'Emily described Greg Nolan and hinted that he needs watching. Did we get a run down on him from the agency?'

Dwight frowned. 'He came to us when we were away in Texas and was cleared, as he was a relative of the gardener who came here four years ago, before I was appointed. Maybe I'll see his references and I can have a quiet word with Chris to see if he's kosher.' He laughed. 'Does Emily think he steals our roses? He's strictly outdoor staff and doesn't come into the house.'

'Wanna bet? I know it's my own fault for leaving things about, and I dismissed them as being mislaid for a while, but I have missed a rather nice scarf pin and now I think of it, maybe other small trinkets and a new leather purse.'

Dwight rang for his secretary. 'I need to see all the files on our personal staff,' he said. 'I think Chris needs upgrading and there might be other changes so to be fair I'll see them all.'

The girl beamed her wide toothpaste advertisement smile. 'Do you want me to go through them? There's quite a pile.'

'No, just stack them here and go off duty. I'll have them put away when I've glanced at them.'

'Oh dear!' Bea was shamefaced when the files were put on the wide desk. 'I didn't mean to make a lot of work for you, Darling.'

'For me?' He smiled sweetly. 'Them who stirs a hornets' nest flushes out the critters and clears up afterwards. I'll let you eat dinner first and then you can get stuck in, but you need only look at the ones who have been here for less than a year.'

'We could do with Mick here,' Bea said with a sidelong glance at Emma.

'Don't you dare! Mick and Eileen are ours and they actually enjoy working for us.'

Emma grinned. 'America is far too strange and dangerous for Eileen, and Mick doesn't like 'abroad'.'

'I admit I tried to outbid you but they are a boring couple who don't know what would be good for them.' Dwight chuckled. 'They looked at me as if I was asking them to stab you in the back and I backed off sharpish.'

'Remember how we did most things together, Sweetie?' Bea dumped a pile of folders in front of Emma and began to sort out the individual dossiers. 'Most of them have been here for years and Dwight trusts them, but there were seven new appointments this year, mostly outdoor staff, since we needed a helipad, and extra fences round new ground that was requisitioned for a pool, and changing rooms and extra quarters for male staff if they live in.'

'Is this the one we want?' Emma held up a slim folder with 'Greg Nolan' written on the cover. 'Lovely name. Sounds like a film star.'

Bea took it and frowned. 'Not much inside; just a letter from a priest saying he knew Greg to be a good worker and another

291

from our own gardener saying that Greg is his second cousin and a good worker.'

'No history of education or former employers unless he worked for the priest ever since he left school. Comparing this with other folders, they are far more detailed and the applicants obviously were interviewed before being accepted.'

'This one was employed at roughly the same time and we have much more detail about him.'

'We can put the rest back in the office but I think I'll check with the priest. Too late now, but I'll telephone in the morning. I think I'll do this. Dwight wouldn't want the staff to think he was checking them out as if he thought they were not all they professed to be.'

She made a note of St Saviour's seminary, New York City, and just after nine the next day, she contacted the right number.

'Nolan? I do recall a Nolan here.' The voice was brisk and Bea knew that this was a man who had no time to waste on idle talk. 'What's he doing now? No trouble?'

'I am making sure that all our employees

are as their references state and his name was in our files with very little detail apart from two letters, one of which is yours.'

'Mine? Now let me think. I wrote a note to the owner of a café after he left here and when they rang for more details as they noted my address, I said what was true, that he was a good worker. No need to say more as I thought he'd have gotten over his earlier troubles. I hoped he was completely rehabilitated and I heard no more of him. Is he still washing dishes and slinging hash?'

'No.'

'He knows he must get in touch with the authorities if he changes employment. Are you about to employ him?'

'He has been an undergardener at the home and offices of an important Air Force family for six months.'

'Is he in trouble?'

'I'm not sure. We have no proof of any misdemeanour but a few small items are missing from the residence. You seemed to think I would know about you and your seminary.'

'I run a unit to train juvenile delinquents

and show them the right path. Nolan did time in a centre for petty crime and before that was in a home for young offenders.'

'Oh!'

'It would seem that he slipped through the net, Madam. I hoped he would make out and maybe he can if he knows he is being watched.' It was almost a plea. 'I could talk to him and warn him if that would help, but he must be stopped if he is pilfering again.'

'He works hard in the gardens and is well liked. May I leave this with you, Father, at least for a few weeks and we can talk again.' Bea gave him details of Dwight's rank and address and telephone number so that Nolan could be contacted. 'If possible I'd like to keep him in our employ but he must be told the alternative to complete honesty on our property.'

'I think that you have handled people like this, Madam. I sense experience and caring. Many would dismiss him as worthless when he might respond to encouragement.'

'A ward of soldiers is a great education, Father.'

He laughed. 'I see I need tell you nothing.

I am pleased to talk to you. Maybe we can save the lad, as I think he has no real vice.'

Emma nodded when she heard about the conversation. 'We met a few like him at Heath Cross, a bit weak but not really bad.'

'All I have to do is to sell the idea of keeping him to Dwight, reminding him that we have no proof that he stole anything.'

'It's a lesson to take nothing for granted and to lock up all treasures. It must be tempting to see something pretty and never have a hope of owning anything as good.'

A few days later, a large brown envelope with no note inside arrived for Mrs Miller, hand delivered, containing every small trinket that Bea had missed over the past few weeks and she told Dwight that she had found what she thought she had lost.

Nolan and the gardener seemed embarrassed when she made a point of going into the garden to talk to them. Bea made no mention of having spoken to the priest but suggested that they might like to enter a flower show and maybe earn a prize and a lot of local fame. 'You really like your job, don't you, Nolan?'

'Yes, Ma'am.'

'Then make sure you keep it. We'll help you if you get into difficulties, and Mr Miller would like you to enter shows and be able to take people round the gardens.'

'Greg works hard, Mrs Miller, and in many ways he's better than I am.'

Bea saw the sweat on the gardener's brow and the anxiety as Nolan shifted uneasily, half expecting to be sent away, and she thought of many boys who became drifters after being demobbed, because they were not given a chance.

'I trust you to do a good job here and to keep your record clean,' she said solemnly. 'That's all, and I look forward to seeing you hold a challenge cup one day. Did you know that a winner has to return the cup each year but is given a small real silver copy to keep for ever? Something good of your own, that you could earn, if these roses are anything to go by.'

Nolan flushed and to hide his relief and emotion bent to cut a rose which he handed to her. 'This is a new hybrid and I could show this next month if that's okay.'

Bea turned away. She smelled the open rose and admired the closed bud with it. 'Keep me informed, but do that through Chris, as you are not indoor staff and must never come into the main building.' She strode over the terrace and into the house aware that they knew how close Nolan had been to dismissal and that it was up to him to remain in the garden he had grown to love.

'Sorted?' Dwight asked.

Bea kissed him. 'Nolan had a little trouble as a boy but now he wants to concentrate on making the Miller garden famous.

'You'd better be right,' he replied ominously.

'Don't worry, Chris will keep him in line and he does grow wonderful roses.' She laughed. 'I haven't lost the touch, Dwight. I mentally wore a starched apron and I think he's scared of me.'

'Aren't we all?'

Fifteen

'So this is where they had the Boston Tea Party. It all looks very peaceful and civilised now,' Paul commented.

'Why does it remind me of home?'

'The trams. We are getting rid of ours but they are wise enough to leave them and make a tourist attraction of them. It really is a lovely city.'

'I wish that Rose was here.'

Paul regarded her with an indulgent smile. 'We did agree not to say that more than five times a day. She's perfectly happy with the other children and most of the time here she'd be bored.' He sighed with contentment. 'Make the most of this time together. When did we sit outside a café in the sun, drinking really good coffee and having the leisure to explore on our own?'

'In that case, Mr Energetic, finish that coffee and follow me. I have a leaflet that shows a route through the city, taking in all the old buildings here.'

'Really ancient monuments? Those I must see.'

'Stop being superior. I know they have nothing to touch our cathedrals and castles but to the Americans anything over two hundred years old is historic. The native Indians have a long history but not in elaborate buildings. Nothing here is older than a couple of hundred years, but old by American standards and most dating from the time of the Pilgrim Fathers.'

'She'd love the squirrels,' Paul remarked as a scurry of grey squirrels swung along the branches overhead. 'But not this.' They went into the old courthouse and Emma shivered. Inside it was dark and forbidding and the portraits of long-dead dignitaries, dour-faced and dressed in the plain sombre clothes of the Puritans seemed to accuse anyone who entered the solemn place.

'They look very ... hard.'

'It was a hard life. It took courage to leave their homes for a foreign country, in spite of the fact that they suffered persecution in

England and the Netherlands. Many died during the first year after the pilgrims landed in America and these pictures date from that period. The harshness of their own laws came with them and their religion was based on self-sacrifice and discipline and frugality, so they reflect the harshness of the times. Later we may see relics of the Civil War and everywhere there will be signs of the struggles of a new nation.'

'It's good to be out in the sunshine. How do we cross the river to Cambridge again? Cambridge, America, on the River Charles, and not Cambridge, England on the River Cam.'

'There's a bridge or ferry. It's easy. You could come back here while I'm lecturing,' Paul suggested. 'I don't want you to be bored.'

'That's all settled,' Emma said firmly. 'I shall, as they say here, have a ball. They think of everything. I am to be shown over Harvard University tomorrow and then I have lunch with one of the women professors. I *might* spare you time tomorrow afternoon, and we have the big reception with the members of the faculty in the evening.' Her eyes sparkled. 'I'm enjoying this, and someone promised me that he'd take me on the river the next day.'

'You certainly made a few friends last night at the party. Who is your ferry man? Does he know you are married, and is he bigger than me? Do I have to worry?'

Emma giggled. 'He's enormous but very muscle-bound and he got the idea that I like boat racing as I know Cowes and I have been to Henley.'

'He'll make you cox for an eight.'

'Heaven forbid. You don't think that he meant that kind of boat ride? I thought more like a punt and a gentle drifting down by the banks with a nice cup of tea after it.'

'As you said, this isn't Cambridge, England. No lazy punts and picnic baskets under the willows. Did you bring any slacks with you, and a waterproof? Play your cards right and he may take you tenpin bowling for afters.'

'I knew I should have stayed with Bea.'

'We have time to sit and watch the squirrels for half an hour. This break is good for everyone. Bea was delighted to have Rose to stay with the children and you needed to be with me. We do need an oasis of calm and being together alone,' Paul said gently.

'It's wonderful, and I feel guilty because I don't feel guilty about leaving Rose. You're right. It's wise to make her more in-dependent and that goes for Bea, too. We know we can go back home after the tours, but she can never do that. This is her home now and England will be her place for holidays and visiting friends.'

'She has been a bit clingy which isn't like Bea.' Paul grinned. 'Dwight and I agree that memory lane has a lot to answer for. Bea's good memories began when she was at the Home in Bristol and you all had an effect on her.'

'That place had an effect on all of us and a little suffering is a great means of making bonds! Beatties and Heath Cross were important in many ways.'

'People were important too.' His eyes were dark and the flecks of gold were dormant.

Emma tucked her hand into the angle of

his arm and looked up at his face. 'Guy was important. I would never have met you unless I knew him, and for that alone, I owe him thanks. He helped me to grow up, but the grown-up Emma needed *you*.'

'Thank you for that.' His voice was husky. 'I had been waiting for you all my life and I still can't believe my luck in finding you.' He kissed her tenderly, then laughed. 'Did you see the disapproving look that statue gave us? We'd better be on our way before he condemns us to an afternoon in the stocks for kissing in the park.'

A small ferry took them over the River Charles and they walked along the river bank beneath the trees in the waterside park until they reached the pleasant apartment put at their disposal by the University authorities. Young men swooped along the riverside paths on roller skates or rowed small, elegant skiffs on the river.

Paul showed their identity cards to the janitor of the block of apartments and Emma realised why they had been asked for passport photographs before they reached Harvard. 'Better than our wartime identity cards,' Paul decided. 'I never thought they were 100 per cent safe as they had no picture. Anyone could use them.'

'Bea said that ID cards are used to check on undesirable visitors to important places and to make sure that anyone under twenty-one can't buy alcohol. They are strict about that here and if a boy who is well built and looks as if he is old enough to buy spirits tries to buy some without showing that he is old enough, the licensee will demand to see his ID if he is suspicious. Looking at all those huge lads rowing, I can see that a real check is essential, as many of them look older but may be only seventeen or younger.'

'It's all those steaks and chickens they ate while we were strictly rationed but I wonder if they are any healthier than we were?'

'The boffins now say that we were healthier during rationing than we had been for decades. Even though supplies were scarce, everything was divided evenly and everyone took their complete rations in case they missed something to which they were entitled. The free orange juice and cod liver oil did wonders for children.'

'Some people managed to get extras.'

'The black market added something at a price, but not many people could afford to buy illegal supplies at inflated prices. Hard work and hunger made most food palatable, except for the fish cakes we had at Heath Cross, mostly potato with a fish bone to show that fish was mentioned in the recipe!'

'I doubt if Aunt Emily ever went short but if she did, at least she could make her food edible.'

'She was lucky to have her doctor friend handing over farm produce from grateful patients, but I know that even when she was tired after running the British Restaurant she often cooked and gave away pies and good soup to a lot of needy families. My mother would fry sausages until they lost their flavour and serve them with boiled potatoes but Aunt Emily would make really good toad-in-the-hole with onion sauce. I learned a lot from her. She taught me to make omelettes from dried eggs and they weren't at all bad if they were cooked quickly and served at once.' Emma laughed.

'We probably were more healthy, as we had no chance to put on weight and that awful National loaf was full of calcium and added vitamins, but I remember the first time I tasted really good white bread after years without it. It was wonderful.'

'And now we have anything we like over here. It seems ridiculous that meat is still rationed in England after all this time.' Paul grinned. 'All this and yet I don't really want a steak. Do you know what I want for lunch? The unattainable!'

'Is there such a thing?'

'British fish and chips, with salt and vinegar and crisp batter.'

'We had very good fish with Bea and Dwight,' Emma smiled. 'Very elegantly served but I know what you mean and Bea pines for it too.' She looked dreamy. 'Fresh, and very hot, with chips fried in dripping and wrapped in greaseproof paper and newspaper.'

'You are in America now,' Paul pointed out sternly. 'When offered it, you'll eat a hamburger and like it.' He sighed. 'Time to collect my notes and try to look like a very important English psychiatrist, but this lecture is a short one and will be an introduction to the main one tomorrow. Why not sit in this time? It will be no different from the times when you sit in and guard me from my nymphos.'

She raised her eyebrows. 'Like that is it? Maybe I'd better come along.'

'I'm not sure. Maybe I'm getting paranoic but there's a group of first-year girl students who followed me around after I'd been over to see the head of studies.'

'Freshers,' she corrected him, 'or bobby soxers if you prefer.' Emma tried to see her husband through the eyes of vulnerable students and laughed. 'I think they see you as a film star, or it's the same image. They adore male British voices and you do look good in that suit. They see very few men dressed as smartly here. Few of the staff wear neckties, and as for jackets, well! Maybe the local baseball team will come back from their tour and the girls will wave streamers and pom poms at them. You'll have your nose out of joint.'

'Sooner the better,' he replied with feeling.

'I'll protect you and be the perfect possessive house-wife. I can let them know that however much they feel the need, you do not take private patients to examine their fragile libidos.'

The lecture hall was vast and the many-tiered auditorium was almost full when Emma sat in the front row and Paul left her to find his way onto the platform.

'Isn't he cute?' Emma realised that the slightly overblown wife of the head of the language school who she had met briefly the evening before was referring to Paul. 'I wish he was here forever. I could eat him.' She stared at Emma and seemed envious. 'You are his wife?'

'That's right and I agree. He's sweet enough to eat.' Emma smiled in a friendly way to avoid embarrassing the woman who now regarded her with speculation.

'You're very wise, Honey. If he was mine I'd not let him out of my sight. I shall attend all his lectures.'

'You are studying psychiatry?'

'Not me. I just love to watch good-looking guys, hear wonderful voices and dream,' she admitted cheerfully and Emma decided that she must tell Paul that it wasn't only the teens who lusted after his body!

It soon became apparent that most of the audience was hooked on the subject and the introductory talk about early signs of mental instability in children made a great impression. The time allotted for the talk was overtaken by questions and more questions and the applause, when at last Paul sat down, was prolonged and spontaneous. Emma smiled. He had never expected such a welcome, but then he was always surprised how interested people were when he talked to them.

'Well done,' she whispered, when he came from the platform and sat beside her while the chairman read out the programme for the next day. 'Oh dear!'

The woman's voice was saccharine sweet as she reached across to speak to Paul. 'Doctor, I did enjoy your talk and I want you and your lovely wife to come to dinner with us tomorrow. Just a few friends who are dying to meet you.'

Emma assumed a formal expression and

took her diary from her purse. 'What a pity,' she said, as if she meant it. 'Not a single gap, I'm afraid. Dr Sykes has to attend a formal dinner tomorrow and he has a very full schedule until we leave in a few days' time.' She looked sad. 'I feel they are working him far too hard and that leaves little time for enjoying the company of people he meets during the lecture tour.'

Paul just smiled and nodded.

'If you are free now, Paul,' Emma continued, 'we ought to be on our way. The Professor is expecting us and then we have to dress for the reception.' She extended a hand to the woman who now looked very disappointed. 'It's been so nice talking to you.'

Paul shrugged as if he was making a sacrifice, murmured a goodbye, then shook the woman's hand and followed Emma from the hall. 'You are indispensable! You even remembered to say "skedule" and who is this professor I am meeting now?'

'I lied,' Emma said complacently. 'Did you see the others who were homing in on us to lionise the bestlooking man they've seen this side of Christmas?'

'Doctors don't get this treatment in England.'

'You do but Mick and I protect you, you poor innocent, but the women here are far more liberated and pushy. I think we have to abandon the walk we promised ourselves and settle for tea in the apartment before we dress for dinner.'

'We've plenty of time. Don't walk so fast!'

'Three girls with a lot of determination are heading our way.' Emma saw that one pretended to fall over and sat on the tarmac. 'Whoops! Don't look back, Paul. Keep going and I'll meet you in the lodge.'

Emma turned as one of the girls ran towards her. 'My friend fell down and I think she needs a doctor. She's hurt her ankle,' she said breathlessly, her face flushed, but not with anxiety as she gazed towards the doorway through which Paul had taken sanctuary.

'Maybe I can help. I am a registered nursing sister and far more likely to know what to do than Dr Sykes, as he isn't an accident doctor. He treats the mind and the nervous system.'

'She wants to see the doctor.'

'I'll ask the janitor to ring for a University medic,' Emma offered, but the girl looked sulky and her glance could have curdled milk.

'It's no good, he's gone,' she called and her friend made a miraculous recovery and walked away.

'I knew you had a healing touch,' Paul said, when she joined him in the lodge, 'but this is wonderful. You just speak to them and they walk away completely cured! Even Aunt Emily isn't that clever.'

'If you tease me I'll let you loose with the lions in future,' she warned. 'Film stars and other celebrities must suffer all the time.'

'That's why so many of them need shrinks,' Paul said wryly.

'Dwight says that you could make a fortune here.'

'If I set up here I'd need my own head examined.'

'Being here hasn't changed your mind?'

'Don't look so anxious. I love my home and my country and although I find

America fascinating, it could never be home to me.'

'Poor Bea.'

'Not at all. They are rich enough to have a *pied-à-terre* back home and another on the French Riviera if they wanted that and now Bea knows that transatlantic travel is easier she will come back more often.'

Emma smiled happily. 'We can come over again, too.'

'I want to talk about that. I have been offered a series of talks next year, based on Harvard, with a house and all the trimmings.' He watched her face. 'We would be independent and the house would be big enough to have guests of our own choosing, but we would be here for three months. They tried to make it six months but I reminded them that I have my own work in London and we agreed on three months.'

'They are trying to make you stay here,' Emma remarked shrewdly.

'I did gather that they had considered it, but we could never give up what we have built and the people who mean a lot to us.'

'Three months is possible,' Emma said

slowly. 'If we told Bea that we'd be back soon, it might make a difference to her. What do you think, Doctor?'

'When we arrived, I was worried about her, and when Mark was lost I thought she'd need my help. Underneath her usual bright aplomb, she still has patches of insecurity, but if she knows that we shall not lose touch it will help a lot.'

'Her father and Miranda are there now and she has built up a good relationship with him at last.'

'Not the same. She has only to feel miserable about something trivial and the past could hit her again. She was very insecure when her parents virtually rejected her during the war. She needed them until she made new friends, like you. Now she is fine with Dwight and the children but she still needs good friends.' Paul regarded her seriously. 'It's a two-way thing. You need her, and if we have only one child, Rose will need companions. Eileen's little girl is fine for a playmate but Rose does seem to prefer boys.'

'Mark in particular. He is good for her. He

makes her share and doesn't let her have her own way all the time.'

'So, shall I accept? The practice will stand it as we seem to have acquired someone who might become a full partner on our return. I spoke to Mick yesterday. He sounded very cheerful and he really likes Robert Forsyth.'

'You didn't let me speak to him!'

'There wasn't time. The office here said there was a gap for a transatlantic business call and would I like it, so of course I took the opportunity of getting in touch with Mick, on official business.' He grinned. 'Hardly office hours. It was midnight over there.'

'Accept the offer. It sounds exciting and we shall be able to see a lot more of America.' Emma bit her lip. 'When would we see Aunt Emily?'

'If you consider that we see her only two or three times a year, it will make no difference and it's becoming easier to get in touch by phone. Why are you smiling?'

'I like the idea of being able to make my own tea in a proper pot with real tea and not have to use these bags on the end of string. It didn't seem worth buying loose tea as we are here for such a short time, but if we had a house...'

'Maybe a service flat would be better if only to stop you baking and cooking for an army!'

'I shall remember that when you grumble about American sponge cake and sigh for good rich fruit cake.'

'Ah! that's different. You may cook that if only for Dwight.' He sounded generous and she gave him a dirty look. 'Get changed and meet the intellectuals. We are invited to a film show after dinner.'

'A strange foreign film with subtitles and lots of deep meaning?' Emma asked apprehensively. 'I saw the poster advertising it.'

'Of course not! That's for the young and earnest and those who haven't acquired a bit of taste.'

'So what have we to suffer?'

'You remember during the war when dubious characters came a lot too close and whispered that they had something off-ration to sell? One of the professors made a suggestion like that to me.'

She giggled. 'That sounds compromising. What was it? A visit to a brothel or a blue film?'

'Nothing that would have me drummed out of the Boy Scouts. A genuine 'Saint' film starring Tom Conway with the mellifluous voice and the smoothy manner.'

'Don't look so disgusted. I think he's lovely and so does Mrs Bristow. I shall tell her when I get back.'

I shall buy you popcorn and promptly fall asleep.'

'That's America, God's own country! I love it.'

Sixteen

It was good to be sleeping in the wide comfortable bed again and to hear the early morning giggles of the children as they tapped on the bedroom door to see if they were awake.

'Hush! You can see them after you've washed and dressed. No, Mark, they don't want to see you in your cowboy gear.' Jan sounded anxious and her voice receded along the corridor as she persuaded the children to go with her.

'What luxury,' Paul said, and yawned. 'Do you think Jan would come back with us?'

'Bea would go mad,' Emma said equably, 'but I could get used to having a really good nanny for Rose.'

'Seems a waste just for an only child.' He drew her closer and Emma snuggled against his bare chest. 'It was quite a "home-coming",' he added. 'They did everything but put the flags out and fire a twenty-one gun salute; and we made love.'

'Looking back it seems that we were away for ages, but now I feel that we can pick up the threads as if it was only yesterday that we went to Boston.'

'Before the children burst with energy and the desire to show us all their new toys, thanks to Miranda and Bea's father, we'd better get moving.'

'It was a good time,' Emma said quietly. 'A time to meet new faces and a time to think clearly, away from everyday events.'

'Rose seems happy and didn't really miss us.' Paul touched her cheek gently. 'She'll miss the others when we go home.'

A soft glow made Emma's cheeks bright and her voice was tender. 'I had time to think of the future. We met a lot of people of our own age group and enjoyed it, and Rose did the same. We needed that and I knew that she must have a companion.'

'And so?' His eyes seemed to grow bigger and the flecks of gold were there again.

Emma took a deep breath. 'Last night I took no precautions and it will stay that way.

Maybe we shall have no more children but I think we could now. Stella said that Rose's birth made another baby possible and warned me against leaving too big an age gap.' She laughed. 'At least I can face her and say I am trying.' She examined her reflection in the long cheval mirror. 'Can you bear to see me fat and ugly again?'

'You were never that,' he replied with feeling. 'I'm not surprised, as I know we saw our future more objectively when we were away and this is the natural outcome.'

'*Mummy!*'

'Ouch! Next time do try to have one with a softer voice.' Paul opened the door and picked up the laughing child. 'I want my breakfast,' he said and kissed the warm cheek before he put her down.

'Mark says he wants to come home with us when we go to England.'

'His mummy couldn't spare him,' Emma said firmly. 'But we'll think of something.'

'I can make time for coffee before I do some work,' Dwight said. 'My, you two look really good. Kinda smug. I know the feeling.' He leaned back in the patio chair and grinned. 'We had a good night, too. Nothing like hitting the sack early and having a good night.'

'Shut up,' Bea said firmly, but she had the same glow that Emma knew surrounded her too. 'Must be the weather.'

Jan walked past with the children dressed in swimming things and huge inflatable armbands, heading for the pool. Bea took another muffin and piled English marmalade on it. 'They'll be in there for hours,' she said comfortably. 'Jan loves it, too, so that lets me out.'

'I can't sit here forever. I must sort out my clothes if you say we leave for the mountains tomorrow.'

'Relax. I've told the new girl to do your laundry and she'll pack your bags ready for the next lot. She acted as Miranda's maid and enjoyed it so she might as well do the same for you. There's no need for you to feel guilty.' Bea shrugged. 'There are lots of very nice people without jobs and if we can help out it's good from both sides.'

Paul and Dwight left to sort out their individual appointments. Paul said he'd see them later as he had a lecture to give after lunch.

'Johnny and Avril missed you more than Rose did,' Bea said.

'That's because Rose and Mark are so close,' Emma replied. 'You'll be relieved to hear that I have already refused his offer to come back with us!'

'If he gets too bad, I may put him in a parcel and send him over to you.'

'Bea! You have that Siamese cat with the cream expression. That usually means you are plotting, or you have a secret that you are dying to tell me but want to make me edgy first. What do you know that I don't? Are you coming over to visit us soon?'

'In a month or so. That's a promise.'

'And what else?'

'Nothing.' Bea was all wide-eyed innocence but her smile was affectionate and malicious at the same time, and Emma was suspicious.

'There is something.'

'Have some more coffee.'

'I've finished, thank you. Is it something that Paul knows but I don't?'

'I doubt it. Come on, I want to see the cup that Nolan won for his roses. I promised to take pictures and when we come to the island again, I've begged cuttings from Aunt Emily's old moss rose tree. Nolan has never seen a moss rose and it would be a sensation if he grew it here.'

'Moss roses? When did you talk to Aunt Emily about roses?'

'Don't be jealous. She's my honorary aunt and she likes to have a chat without you listening in.'

'That's the second time you've hogged the phone and given me no chance to talk to her. When did you phone?'

'Dwight arranged another link and just because you were living it up in Boston was no reason for me to miss out on the call!'

'How was she?' Emma sighed. 'She's one of the reasons I could never move to another country. She's my rock.'

'And mine,' Bea said quietly. 'She's the aunt and mother I never had and I owe her a great deal.'

'How was she?' Emma repeated.

'Fine, but busy helping to prepare for

George's wedding. She hopes that little Clive will stay with her when you go there. She said he would be company for Rose ... that is until he has his own brother.'

'Rose loves Clive.'

'Aunt Emily knows that but has a feeling that Rose needs her own brother.' She looked at Emma with the sideways glance that Emma called shifty.

'So what did she say?' Emma's pulse began to race but she remained calm, unable to tell if she felt elated or full of a strange dread.

'She wore her witch's hat,' Bea said.

'Too much whisky in her tea.'

'No, she wanted to talk to me about you. By the way I've saved a lot of Mark's clothes that are hardly worn and some are things you can't buy in London.'

'You may need them.'

'No, *you* may need them.'

Emma's voice was a whisper. 'She said that?'

'Among other things, she said that Rose is like you and getting more so but the boy will be Paul all over again. Come on, the sun is just right for photos. We have time to see the garden properly without the children larking about and trying to be in each shot.'

Bea gave her a hug and Emma smiled tremulously. After their love-making last night, she knew that anything was possible. 'A hundred or so years ago they'd have burned my sainted aunt at the stake,' she murmured.

'What a waste! I bet the inquisitors would have demanded that she tell them the future first.'

'Mountains are impressive but cold,' Emma said, after the first day in the hills.

'Only the top crags,' Bea protested. 'The lower slopes are green and very pretty and heavenly cool just now after Washington. It almost makes up for being a couple of grass widows but Dwight had to go away to Ontario and Paul has lectures to give in so many places that it would have been very uncomfortable and lonely for you. Men travel faster alone with just a suitcase, and his hosts will take pity on him and swamp him with hospitality as he has no wife to spoil him.' Bea laughed. 'He could have everything, but *everything,* offered to him for his comfort and entertainment.'

Emma looked shocked. 'Women?'

'Of course! Men from some countries expect it and the female company is ... laid on ... if you'll excuse the expression, ready and waiting for it.'

'Has Dwight been offered perks like that?'

'Often very young and nubile but he wouldn't dare.' Bea grinned. 'My comprehensive lectures on the dangers of illicit sex made him squirm with horror. He is a sensitive man under that macho boldness. I also said I'd castrate him if he ever as much as put a hand where it didn't belong and he knows that I would sense it if he ever strayed.'

'After you, how could he think of another woman?'

'Paul must be the same.'

'Paul often has to retreat from women with sex problems. He has a lot of experience of recognising the signs. They aren't mad, and others are so unstable that they long to latch on to a strong and good-looking man. I feel like a Victorian chaperone at times but Mick and I deal with the situation.'

'Mick?'

'He deals with the deviant males. Paul could have a very colourful life if he was that way inclined!'

'Poor darlings. How their ears must be burning. At least we are thinking of them and missing them,' Bea said virtuously.

The children ran down to the chalet and demanded lemonade. Mark wore denim jeans and a bright check shirt and Rose followed close behind, carrying a bunch of wilting wild flowers. Paul would love a son. Mark's cheeks were beginning to freckle and Bea brushed his hair out of his eyes.

'You don't freckle and neither does Dwight.'

Bea smiled. 'Dwight's mother will be pleased. She has freckles, and was complaining that none of our children have family resemblances to her or her husband. Mark, ask Jan to cut your hair. You look like a shaggy sheepdog. Oh, now what have I said? He'll bark all through lunch and make his hair fall over his eyes even more.'

'Girls are easier.'

'Just you wait. What are you going to call him?'

'We aren't about to buy a sheepdog.'

'Funny girl! Aunt Emily needs to talk to you.'

The time passed quickly and Dwight and Paul joined the party for a few days, riding and walking and eating in the open with food cooked over wood fires.

If only the sea was there beyond the trees this would be perfect, Emma thought, but kept her opinions to herself as Bea was in her element.

It was wonderful to be with the family that had meant so much in the past and now seemed even closer, but with this journey Emma's dream had been realised and she felt a quiet calm in the conviction that this dream could go on even when the two families were parted. There would be other times, other meetings, and the children cemented the bonds of friendships.

'When we come to England, I want to take the children to Somerset as well as down to the island. Johnny and Avril need to ride over open country and to learn to use our saddles instead of these armchairs.'

'You are looking forward rather soon.'

'I want them to get used to both countries and to love the English countryside,' Bea told her. 'You may not know this but when I came to America I cried for a week when Dwight wasn't around and I dreaded going back to London in case I refused to come away again.'

'I guessed, and Emily warned me to say nothing to make you homesick,' Emma said dryly. 'It was strange that you should feel homesick. You took enough stuff with you to remind you of London. Our house seemed half empty after you left and Dwight must have been tearing his hair when he saw just how much old furniture you sent over.'

Bea giggled. 'I still sit in that tatty old chair when I feel blue but I found Avril in it one day sucking her thumb and feeling unwanted. There must be more than horsehair in the stuffing.'

'I think that Paul talked to London yesterday and contacted the airport. That

330

means we shall be leaving.'

'It's sad but not all that sad. I can reach out and almost touch you across the ocean in future, and think of the wonderful things we can store up to tell each other.'

'Don't come to the airport. I hate goodbyes, and Mark and Rose could be difficult.'

'He can ride that morning and Rose can take a few small wrapped gifts to undo on the plane.'

'I'll give your love to Aunt Emily and Janey. George is safely married and I can feel free from him completely.'

'When do you see Clive?'

'He will be with Aunt Janey on the island for a while, so I must make time to take Rose there for a day or so and I hope he'll visit us with Aunt Janey and help to fill the gap that Mark will leave.'

Everything was suddenly rushing into the future and Emma hardly drew breath before they landed at London Airport. America faded away, but not the dreams she'd discovered and stored in her memory.

She was happy.

A familiar figure waited by their car and Mick waved. 'Welcome back,' he said.

The publishers hope that this book has given you enjoyable reading. Large Print Books are especially designed to be as easy to see and hold as possible. If you wish a complete list of our books please ask at your local library or write directly to:

Magna Large Print Books
Magna House, Long Preston,
Skipton, North Yorkshire.
BD23 4ND

This Large Print Book for the partially sighted, who cannot read normal print, is published under the auspices of

THE ULVERSCROFT FOUNDATION